Autumn's
BLOOD

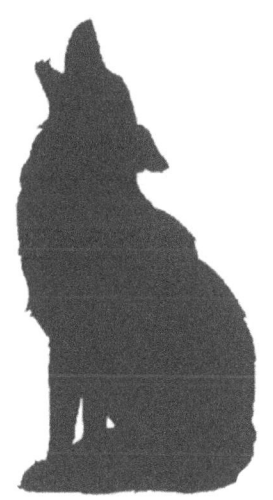

THE SPIRIT SHIFTERS BOOK ONE

MARISSA FARRAR

AUTUMN'S BLOOD
The Spirit Shifters: Book One

Copyright © 2013 Marissa Farrar

Warwick House Press

Edited by Wade-Staten Services
Cover art by Marissa Farrar

eBook ISBN: 978-0-9928504-5-6
Paperback ISBN: 978-0-9928504-9-4

FOR MY FAMILY

CHAPTER ONE

BLAKE WOLFCOLLAR FOLDED his arms across his massive chest and bit down on the fury tearing through him. He needed to keep control of his emotions. Now more than ever. Losing his grip on himself would mean exposing his true identity to the people who wanted to control his kind.

Bulletproof glass separated a team of men—which included him—from the three people held captive. Further sheets of glass divided the prisoners, deliberately done in order for the detainees to be able to witness each other's torment. In each of the glass cubicles, a solitary metal chair was bolted to the floor. The prisoners—a woman in her mid-thirties, a man of about the same age, and a boy in his teens—had each been handcuffed to the chairs. To any outsider, the people could have been a young family, but Blake knew they'd never laid eyes upon each other until they'd been brought to the facility.

The government building towered above their heads, but they weren't being held above the city. This part of the compound was buried several stories beneath ground level, preventing anyone who shouldn't be there overhearing what was going on.

His superior, and friend, Peter Haverly, glanced over his shoulder to where Blake stood, his back to the two-inch-thick metal door which led to the elevator providing access to the rest of the building. Haverly's eyes widened at him briefly, accompanied by a slow shake of his head.

Keep your cool.

Blake pressed his lips together and glanced away. He understood what Haverly was telling him—don't get involved, stay quiet for the good of their kind—but he wasn't known for his self-control.

Maxim Dumas, a silver-haired head of *Operation Pursuit*, pressed a button located on the control panel in front of him. He leaned forward and spoke into a small microphone. "We know what each of you is. If you simply change for us now, we won't have the need to use force."

A growl threatened to rumble from Blake's throat, but he managed to swallow it down. The blunt ellipses of his nails dug into the intricate tribal tattoo etched into the bulk of his bicep. He forced himself to loosen his grip and ran a big palm over his head, his dark hair buzzed military short. He had no way of telling Dumas that the man, woman, and boy were unable to change at will without blowing his cover. Most spirit shifters only fused with their spirit guides in moments of intense stress, pain, or emotions. Of course, what Dumas planned on doing would take these people to such a level, but he would assume they cracked under torture rather than realize the pain was the actual trigger.

The people behind the screen stared at each other, abject fear widening their eyes. Blake recognized the woman's coffee-colored skin, only a shade darker than his own, and her almost-black eyes and long, shiny, dark hair. *Had they taken her from a reservation?* Or was she like him, one of the lucky ones who had managed to escape the poverty and build a new life?

She strained against her bonds. "Who are you? Why are you doing this to us?"

Dumas leaned forward once more. "I don't believe you're in any position to be asking questions, Ms. Lowery. The chair you are strapped to has an electrical current of over a thousand volts attached to its feet. If you don't do as I ask, I will make sure my people start applying that voltage. We'll start off low, but it won't stay that way for long if you don't comply."

"You can't do this!" she cried. "This is abduction, and you're threatening torture! It's against the law."

He leaned forward. "We're outside of the law, Ms. Lowery. Now, I suggest you do as I tell you and change before I get my men to switch on the current."

"Fuck you!"

Dumas turned to the other men and caught Blake's eye. "She's feisty." He nodded approvingly. "I like that."

"What the hell do you people want?" the man yelled, but no one acknowledged him.

Blake knew his background: married for eight years, two children—a boy and a girl—your average American Joe. With the exception of being able to shift into the form of his animal spirit guide. For now, Dumas' attention seemed to be focused on the boy and the woman. Blake didn't doubt the man's time would come.

Dumas turned back. "Do you see the boy sitting in the chamber beside you? How about if he's the one who receives the charge? Do you know what a high electrical current does to the human body, Ms. Lowery? Oh, but wait. You're not exactly human, are you?"

"I don't know what you're talking about."

He laughed. "Why keep denying it?"

Blake clenched his teeth. Dumas was wrong. Spirit shifters were human, at least most of the time. They just had talents unlike the vast majority of their counterparts. Their abilities varied from shifter to shifter. Where some people, like himself, had been chosen by their animal spirits at birth and so could shift at will, the majority were chosen by their spirits later in life, making their powers less.

"Do you know what happens to the body during an electrocution?" Dumas continued. "Your heart will stop; whether that's permanent or simply an arrhythmia, depends on the voltage. Every muscle in your body will go rigid. You will probably bite down on your tongue, possibly severing it. Oh, and because you're not completely strapped down, there is a good chance an arch of electricity will leap from the chair to your body, causing severe burns. Is that what you want to happen to the boy?"

Her gaze darted wildly to the teenager in the room beside her. The boy renewed his struggles, the muscles in his arms popping as he tried to wrench them from the cuffs.

"I can't do what you want me to!" she cried. "It doesn't work like that!"

A sly smile quirked Dumas' lips. "So you admit there is something you can do?"

Tears welled in her dark eyes. She looked between the boy on one side of her and the man on the other. The man's jaw tensed and he gave his head a slight shake.

Blake took a deep breath, trying to disguise his reactions to the scene playing out in front of him, allowing the air to exhale slowly through his nose. He wanted nothing more than to leap at Dumas and rip him from the control panel and set the other shifters free, but he couldn't. This thing was bigger than three people. He'd need to find a way to release them, but he'd need to do it later, when he could disguise his identity. Being in the middle of this thing allowed him to learn of the government's plans, even if it was simply by eavesdropping on conversations. Haverly was also privy to most of the secret conversations, but not all of them. Blake was used as muscle for whatever Dumas wanted, and the man tended to keep him around. Learning more about the progress of *Operation Pursuit* was the most important thing. At times like this, he needed to remember that.

Dumas' head cocked to one side. "Time's up." He gave a nod to the man sitting beside him, a technical guy Blake only knew as Miller. The man returned the nod and flicked a switch.

The boy went rigid in his chair, his fingers curling, his knuckles turning white from the pressure of his grip on the arms of the chair. The shock was small and he fell limp after only a couple of seconds, but he groaned, his head lolling forward.

The woman stared at the boy in alarm and then back at the two-inch-thick glass. Due to the one-way mirrors positioned on her side, she was unable to see her captors. "What the hell do you think you're doing?"

"Are you going to do what we want?"

"I can't! How many times do I have to tell you?"

"Then we'll increase the voltage."

Dumas gave Miller another nod and the man twisted a dial on the console and flicked the switch once more.

Instantly, the boy bucked in the chair, his back arching, his narrow chest thrusting out. His eyes rolled in his head, flashing the forked red of his eyeballs. He jerked, his hands once again tightening around the arms of the chair as a higher voltage of electricity shot through his young body.

"No! Stop!" the woman screamed. "You're hurting him."

The man said nothing, but resumed his efforts to get free. Miller flicked the switch and the current died, the boy dropping limp in his chair.

Blake's heart lodged in his throat. Was the boy dead? No, his eyes flickered open and he started to groan.

Dumas pushed the button for the microphone. "That was nothing. We can go a lot higher."

She pounded her fists against the metal armrest of her chair. "I can't do it at will! Why won't you listen to me?" She paused, her eyes widening. "Electrocute me! If you electrocute me, I might be able to change for you. I'll try, honest I will."

Blake didn't want to see either of them electrocuted, but the woman might be stronger. The boy would have turned by now if he had the power to do so. Blake could only assume the reason he hadn't was because his connection with his spirit was weak, and possibly the electric current had done nothing to help. Either that or he was strong enough to resist.

But Dumas shook his head. "I'm the one who makes the decisions around here. I don't do bargaining. Especially not with a bunch of freaks."

"Perhaps her idea is a good one."

The three men sitting at the control panel turned at Blake's voice.

Dumas appraised him with his cool, blue eyes. "And why would you say that?"

"Let her feel what the boy is suffering. Maybe if she experiences the sort of pain he's in, it'll help her make her decision."

Dumas narrowed his eyes and opened his mouth to speak, but Haverly interrupted. "I think Sergeant Wolfcollar might be onto something. We need to change things up a bit."

Dumas looked between the two men and gave a slow nod. "Very well." He turned to the man controlling the current. "A thousand volts to the woman."

Miller nodded and pushed his wire rim glasses higher on his nose. He reached out and switched on the electricity. The brunette went rigid, her eyes wide. She juddered in the chair as the volts raced through her body. Her fingers curled, her knuckles white, her eyes bulging from her head.

Dumas gave the nod and the other man flicked the switch back again.

The electricity stopped and she fell forward, slumped in the chair. Her whole body heaved as she breathed in deep gasps, her hair falling over her face.

As they watched, the muscles in her back rippled beneath her t-shirt. Her slender biceps bulged, swelling against the material of her clothes.

She lifted her face to them, her dark eyes wide. "It's happening! You need to let me out of these cuffs." She yanked on the shackles on both her wrists and ankles. Blake caught sight of painful red burn marks beneath the metal. He wanted to look away, but duty kept his eyes focused. He was playing a part in this and needed to see it through. His involvement was for the best in the long run.

Dumas laughed. "I think not."

With his stomach sinking, Blake realized what was about to happen. "You need to undo the cuffs. They're too small for her."

Dumas spun around. "They fit perfectly. And what is it to you?"

"They won't be in a minute."

The woman lifted her head and screamed. The sound of bones cracking ricocheted around the small room. She dropped her head again, panting.

Miller's eyes widened behind his glasses, his already pallid face paling further, and he leaned back in his chair. "What the hell?"

This must be his first time witnessing a shift, Blake realized. He wondered if the tech guy would return for a second viewing.

Her hair seemed to shrivel away, as though a flame had been

applied to it, revealing the shape of two ears curling from the top of her head. She lifted her face again, her dark eyes now flashing yellow, but her features were no longer those of an attractive woman. Her canines were white in her elongated jaw, her skin covered in thick, black hair. Her bones cracked, her fingers curling in to create paws, claws piercing through the skin of the second knuckle of her fingers. More short black hair sprouted from the backs of her hands. The thickness of her forearms grew, and Blake looked on in horror, knowing exactly what was going to happen.

The metal rings didn't give with the growth. Instead, her skin, bones, and flesh gave way beneath the restraints, snapping what had previously been her wrists but were now her front legs.

She twisted in her shackles, growling and hissing in agony. Under the cuffs, each limb had been crushed and now hung at painful angles. Though Blake knew she would heal—and heal quickly, it was part of the make-up of their kind—if they didn't get her out of the cuffs right away, her joints would heal at those awkward angles and they would need to be broken again to heal straight.

The team looked on as the bleeding, snarling, still-cuffed black panther twisted in agony behind the glass.

CHAPTER TWO

AUTUMN ANDERSON SMOOTHED down the skirt of her suit and trotted up the stairs toward the entrance. Doors of darkened glass hid whatever lay inside from view. The building looked like any other high-rise in Chicago. With the exception of the lack of signs proclaiming the business housed within its walls. If she'd not been invited here personally, she'd never have known the building was government-owned.

Nerves skittered around her stomach. This wasn't like a regular job interview. She'd been invited here by the head of a department who needed her skills. Assuming she didn't manage to somehow insult the guy or fall flat on her face, the job was hers.

Even so, the mystery surrounding what the job actually involved had her concerned. All they'd told her over the phone was that the information was "classified."

Placing a hand against the smooth, cool glass, she pushed. It didn't budge. Positioned on the wall on either side of her head, cameras, like bionic eyes, swiveled to take in the new arrival. She looked up at them and suppressed the urge to wave.

A sudden voice made her jump. "Please state your name and business."

She glanced around, but found she was still alone. Then she noticed what she hadn't before—a small silver intercom embedded in the wall at head height. There were no buttons to press, so she hesitantly spoke into the circle.

"Umm… My name is Doctor Anderson. General Maxim Dumas is expecting me."

No one responded, but a faint buzz sounded and the door clicked open.

Autumn took a deep breath and stepped through.

Blocking the way was a large metal detector, similar to the type she'd been through at the airport. On either side of the detector stood two large men in blue security uniforms. Her eyes flicked down to the firearms attached to their hips and then back up again, pretending not to either notice or be bothered.

"Doctor Anderson?"

One of the big security guards stepped forward and handed her a security badge. She was surprised to find her name and photo on the card instead of a regular generic visitor badge, though the word *visitor* was printed beneath her name.

She took it and offered him a smile, but the man remained stony-faced. Instead of returning the gesture, he nodded past the detector, toward a set of elevators beyond. "General Dumas is on the twelfth floor."

"Thank you," she said, about to pin the badge to her shirt. The guard picked up a small black tray and offered it in her direction.

She realized what he wanted and dumped the badge, together with her purse, into the tray.

"I'm afraid we'll need your shoes as well."

Feeling faintly ridiculous, she slipped off her sensible heels and added them to the tray. The guard pushed the tray through a scanner and nodded toward the detector again.

Getting the hint, she walked through, half-tensed, expecting it to go off, despite there being no reason for the alarm to sound. When it didn't, she retrieved her belongings and slipped her shoes back on.

"Thanks," she said again and headed toward the elevator. To her right, she spied a long corridor, glass offices positioned either side. The shapes of people moved within, but she wasn't given any time to assess any of her potential colleagues.

"This way please."

She'd expected to go alone, but the burly man had followed her and now gestured directly ahead. She felt overly conscious of his presence close behind her left shoulder. She hit the button for the elevator and the doors slid open. Walking through, she turned around, searching for the control panel. Before she had the chance to find the button for the twelfth floor, the guard leaned in and pressed it for her before retreating.

The doors slid close and Autumn stood in the center, the rise of the car leaving her already nervous stomach behind. Mirrors covered the walls on each side. She gave her reflection a quick assessment, making sure none of her blonde curls had escaped the tight knot at the nape of her neck that she'd wrestled her hair into. One thing she'd learned over the years: no matter how many letters she had after her name, as soon as people saw her, they judged her on her appearance—young, blonde, and female. She had to work her ass off to fight against the stereotype and always tried to appear as sensibly groomed as possible.

The elevator opened onto a corridor. She stepped out, craning her head left and right, trying to figure out which direction to go. Closed doors lined the corridor, but a smartly dressed woman hurried toward her, files clutched in her arms.

"Excuse me? I'm looking for General Dumas' office."

The woman offered her a faint smile. "Last door on the left."

"Thank you."

Autumn hurried in the direction she'd been pointed until she reached the correct door. A bronze plaque with Dumas' name was positioned at eye level. She took another steadying breath and knocked.

"Come in," a voice called.

She pushed open the door and walked through. A man in his fifties with silver hair sat behind a large mahogany desk. He looked up from his paperwork, regarding her with ice-blue eyes. He smiled, though something about the expression didn't quite fit.

The man half rose and leaned across the desk, extending a hand toward her. "Doctor Anderson, I assume."

She took his hand. His grip was cool and firm. "General Dumas," she said. "It's good to meet you."

"You too." He gestured to the chair on the other side of his desk. "Please, take a seat."

She sat opposite, keeping her back straight, her ankles crossed.

"So." He looked down at a folder of notes on the desk. "Doctor Autumn Anderson. Youngest woman to attend Yale and youngest to graduate. PhD in molecular genetics, a second PhD in molecular biology. And now, at the ripe old age of twenty-seven, one of the country's most sought after minds on DNA."

She risked a smile. "I enjoy my work."

"I see your father is also a scientist, a leader in evolutionary biology."

"That's right. I guess you could say my love for science is in the blood."

He lifted his eyes to her. "And your mother?" he inquired, eyebrows lifted.

"She died when I was five years old. I don't really remember her. My father raised me."

"So you and your father must be close?" He offered her no commiseration for her loss.

"We get along, as long as the conversation turns to the topic of work." She wondered why he needed to know all of this, struggling to understand how her often strained relationship with her father had anything to do with what they wanted her to work on now.

"And I see you've had some success splicing and manipulating genes to create new embryos of what could potentially be new species."

"That's correct, though of course, those embryos were never grown any further. That would be against the law. You're not asking me to try to create a new species, I hope, General." There was a teasing tone behind her voice.

He shook his head. "No, of course not. The species I hope you will work on already exists. But what I would like you to attempt to do is manipulate genes to mutate in a certain way in order for one gene to become another."

"So what species is it you're asking me to work on?"

"You don't need to know what it is, you just need to know what result we need. Now, would you like the job, or do I need to find someone else?"

Autumn straightened. "I'm the best in my field. Good luck finding someone else."

"Is that your way of telling me you don't want the job?"

She hesitated. While she knew she'd find another job easily enough, it was never good to piss off the people at the top of the food chain. Plus, she had to admit, her interest had been piqued.

"Not at all, General. If you'd still like me on board, I'd be excited to find out what you have planned."

A slow smile spread across his face. He rose from his chair and extended his hand. She returned the smile and shook his hand once more.

"Then, welcome to the team, Doctor Anderson."

"So when do I start?"

"How does first thing tomorrow morning sound?"

The suddenness startled her, but she didn't have anywhere else to be. "Perfect."

He made his way around the desk to escort her from the room. Before he got the chance, a knock sounded. The door cracked open.

A huge man with caramel skin and piercing dark eyes dwarfed the doorway. Autumn had to stop herself from staring. He wore a tight black t-shirt, and she could just make out the swirls of some kind of tribal tattoo peeping from beneath the material stretching around the bulk of his bicep.

"I'm sorry, General," the man said, his eyes flicking from Maxim Dumas to take in Autumn. "I didn't realize you weren't alone."

Dumas shook his head. "Don't worry, Sergeant. Actually, I'd like you to meet a new member of our team. This is Doctor Autumn Anderson. Autumn, this is Blake Wolfcollar, the head of our security team here."

Wolfcollar… She recognized the name as being Native American. That would explain the beautiful complexion.

The imposing man didn't smile at her. Instead, his dark eyes seemed to bore through her, and Autumn actually felt her heart stutter.

He put his hand out toward her and she took it, her small palm vanishing in his massive fist. The heat of his skin surrounded hers, burning into her as though he had a fever. He locked those intense, almost-black eyes on her and warmth flared to her cheeks.

"Doctor?" he inquired. "Does that mean you've come to assist with our medical problem?" His eyes darted to Dumas.

"Oh, no," she said, wondering what the medical problem was. "I'm not a medical doctor. I'm a molecular geneticist."

"I see. So you've come to work on our shifter problem."

She frowned. "Shifter?"

Dumas cleared his throat. "Autumn hasn't been filled in on that particular part of things. She's working on a need-to-know basis."

Autumn felt herself shrink. So he wanted her on the team, but was clearly expecting her to work with less knowledge about the project than other members. Well, she would have to make sure that changed, but right now she just needed to get her foot in the door. She'd start to make waves later.

Shifter? What the hell is a shifter?

"Anyway," said the man she now knew was called Blake. "We need you down in the … lab, General. There have been some developments."

"I'll be with you in a minute. I'll just escort Doctor Anderson out."

Blake flashed her a measured smile. "Why don't you allow me to see the doctor out?" he said, addressing Dumas, but never taking his eyes off Autumn.

"Very well. Blake will take good care of you, Doctor Anderson. We'll see you back in the morning."

"Absolutely."

The big, imposing man held the door open for her, forcing her to brush past him as she went by. This guy seemed to radiate heat. She'd have sworn she could feel him from here. What would it be like to press the length of her body up against his, with no clothing in the way?

She quickly glanced away, horrified at where the thought had come from.

Walking down the hall, the giant man followed close behind. When she stopped at the bank of elevators, he leaned across her and pressed the button to call the car. His proximity was so close she could almost turn her head and press her face into the solid mass of his shoulder.

They stepped into the elevator, Autumn sneaking glances in the mirrors surrounding them at the man next to her. A square jaw, strong nose with slightly flared nostrils, impossibly dark eyes fringed with even darker lashes. A fine down of soft black hair covered the ridges of his well-muscled arms and she couldn't help but stare as he reached across her once again to hit the floor they needed. They rode in silence and she didn't think she imagined the tension filling the small space. They locked eyes in the mirror and both quickly glanced away. He cleared his throat and the doors pinged open. They stepped out, Autumn just ahead.

The security guards sat behind a desk, the metal detector acting as a barrier between them.

Autumn drew to a stop. "I think I can find my way from here."

He gave her a nod, his dark eyes drilling into hers. "I'm sure you can." But he made no move to head back to the elevator, but instead stood, still staring at her. "So are you looking forward to starting on our project?"

"I would be if I knew a little more about it."

"You will," he said.

She smiled shyly and glanced at the floor, wondering how to make her excuses. For some reason, just a *bye* didn't seem like enough. She found herself drawn to this man, not wanting to leave his side.

"Well, I'm looking forward to telling my roommate about getting the job," she said, realizing she was also telling him she didn't live with a man.

Suddenly he stepped closer, lifted his hand, and placed the side of his index finger against her lips. His skin burned against hers. She was too shocked to react, step away, or tell him not to touch her.

"Our project here is a secret," he said, his voice low. "You mustn't speak of it to anyone."

He seemed to realize the location of his finger and quickly pulled his hand away and took a step back. "Good afternoon, Doctor Anderson."

Flustered, she said, "Good afternoon." She turned and walked from the building, feeling his gaze follow her the whole way.

CHAPTER THREE

BLAKE NEEDED TO run.

Though shifting into his spirit guide's form was always agony, tonight, the need gnawed at him like an addiction. He sensed himself on the brink already, his body filling with the nerve-rattling vibrations that signaled the change.

He knew he could put the urge down to what he'd witnessed with Maxim Dumas and the captive shifters, but for some reason it seemed as if it had more to do with the blonde scientist whose path he'd crossed afterward. He couldn't explain it, but something about her had captured his attention, and it wasn't just the big blue eyes, elfin face, or the way her blonde curls had escaped her hairstyle to brush her long neck. At about five-eight, she was still far shorter than his six-foot-four frame, but she'd appeared strong, a jut to her jaw which had given him the impression that she meant business.

He'd been aware of Autumn being in the room before he'd even knocked on Dumas' door. His keen hearing and sense of smell had been able to detect her, but he'd also been able to send his wolf guide into the room ahead of him. His guide had placed her image in his head, allowing him to observe her before he'd ever come face to face with the new doctor. He needed to learn about her. Her presence could change this whole thing. If she succeeded in her job, the whole world might change.

Blake had left the government building shrouded in guilt about abandoning the three shifters held captive. He wanted so badly to do something to help them, but his hands were tied. Peter Haverly had sensed his mounting frustration and sent him from the building. Though Blake's command over his spirit guide was as strong as his kind got, he still ran the risk of stepping over that boundary and losing control. Both he and Haverly knew they couldn't allow that to happen.

Already, the spirit form of his wolf had headed into the forest. Blake closed his eyes to connect with his guide. The scent of a small animal filled its nostrils and it darted its head that way, tracking the trail. Not that Blake's guide was able to do anything about hunting the prey. Though his wolf, while in spirit form, could sense the world around him, it could not interact or affect it in any way. Only when they morphed together did his spirit get to experience the world for real—taste the hot gush of blood as it killed a meal, rejoice in the scent and feel of the undergrowth as it rolled in dirt and fallen leaves.

This was the reason the spirit guides attached themselves to certain men and women. They got to experience the world as though they were alive. In return, the humans benefited from heightened senses and strength, and got to experience life in another form.

Not all shifters were the same. Some, like him, were chosen by their spirit guides at birth. This was rare and meant he was stronger and more attuned to his spirit than most. His spirit had been a part of him for as long as he'd been on this earth. This made him stronger, faster, and able to shift at will. Others were chosen later in life, so they never became as completely in tune with their guides. These shifters didn't have control over when they shifted, and occasionally they didn't shift at all. Plus, not all shifters, just like not all spirits, were good. Some worked badly, drove their human counterparts crazy, or used them to murder.

Blake had traveled deep enough into the forest now to avoid any accidental happening upon by regular humans. From his own sense of smell, he was certain none were near, and his wolf guide hadn't crossed any.

While the change only took minutes to occur, to Blake it felt like hours, the agony so intense the seconds stretched on. He couldn't risk being found mid-shift. He was all but helpless then, at his weakest point. As both man and wolf, he was big, strong, and feared by most. When not fully in either form, he was as helpless as a newborn.

Pausing in the depths of the forest, he kicked off his boots, leaving them in the dirt. He tugged his t-shirt over his head, enjoying the night's air against his bare skin. Whipping open the buckle of his jeans, he popped the button and shrugged them from his body so he stood naked, surrounded only by trees. Blake closed his eyes once again.

Come to me, he willed. *Be one with me.*

Instantly, he sensed his wolf guide being pulled backward through the ether, like a rush of energy blasting toward him. He stood with his shoulders back, his face lifted to the sky, his fists clenched.

The spirit hit him like a blast of power, knocking him back. He staggered to keep his balance as fire surged through his body, feeling like every nerve ending had been set alight.

Blake roared in pain, his face lifted to the night sky. All around him, roosting birds burst from the trees in a flurry of flapping wings.

The sound of every bone in his body breaking ricocheted like gunshots inside his head. Red-hot splinters of agony pierced every part of his body. He fell to his knees, his head hanging down. He felt his jaw change, jutting forward, his mouth suddenly full of long, sharp teeth. His ears unfolded from the top of his head. Instantly, his hearing became even sharper, the scents of the forest causing his nostrils to flare.

His entire skin prickled as though someone were piercing it with a thousand needles as individual strands of fur sprouted. An ache at the base of his spine signaled the growth of his tail, then the skin split and the new appendage unfurled.

The shift was complete.

Blake hung his head, panting, his tongue lolling from his mouth. Slowly, the final residues of pain began to subside.

He shook his body, like a dog after a swim, sending his fur flying around his rippling muscles.

As a wolf, he stood almost as tall as he did in man form. His beautiful silver fur was streaked with black down his face and body. Blake's muscles burned with strength, and he lowered to a crouch before springing forward. He took off at speed through the forest.

In the back of his mind, he sensed his spirit guide's presence. He experienced such clarity when they became one. Normally, as a human, a part of his mind always seemed to be somewhere else, like a daydream he couldn't shake. But when he and his wolf resided in the same body, the world grew sharper than he'd ever thought possible.

His guide remained quiet, content to simply experience the world for real. Should it need to let Blake know something, it placed the image in his head—*rabbit, human, trap*—and he took steps to either hunt or avoid.

Occasionally, Blake wished they were able to communicate in words, but his guide wasn't human and never had been. It communicated in the only way it knew how—through images and emotions.

Movement came in the distance, in the undergrowth ahead. A skittering of hooves in leaves, the snort of hot air through nostrils. All these things washed over him, the knowledge without even having to see it—a deer, a young buck. He could tell simply by the weight of its movement on the ground and the hormones the animal gave off. The animal had sensed him too, something he knew from the sharp tang of fear pheromones that assaulted his sensitive nostrils.

Blake paused, a moment of uncertainty rippling through him.

Had something else alerted the deer, something else made it skittish?

No, surely he'd have sensed it.

The one drawback of being wolf was no longer having the benefit of a spirit guide to send ahead. When they resided in the same body, his guide became a part of him, and he his guide. The guide was tethered to earth and to the physical bonds which tied them together. He couldn't send it ahead to get a sense of what lay before them.

He smelled the sweat quivering on the deer's flank, the hot gusts of its breath. His wolf guide thrust images into his head—blood, meat, the satisfying lust of the kill—and pushed him onward.

Blake ran through the forest, leaping fallen logs, swerving around trees, breaking through bushes. The deer also ran, hooves drumming a tribal beat against the forest floor. Blake panted; hot breath on a cool night. His muscles were strong and tireless. The deer was still some distance ahead, but he had plenty of time to reach it. This was how wolves hunted, long distance running in order to run their prey to a point of exhaustion and then pounce. Of course, normally, they hunted in a pack, but he was a lone wolf and different from regular wolves. He was bigger—easily four times the size of a regular wolf—with fierce senses and didn't tire so easily. Other factors came into play at supernatural level, such as his ability to heal quickly.

The sudden scent of blood filled the air, a tidal wave of copper and heat. The animal's frightened bleat of terror, the savage tear of flesh.

Blake skidded to a halt, ears pricked, eyes wide. Something had happened to the animal, but what? He slowed his pace and proceeded with more caution.

Underlying the overwhelming stench of blood, he caught the scent of something else—someone else—a scent he'd not come across for several years.

A low growl rumbled from his throat. He lowered his powerful neck and sniffed the ground. Yes, how had he missed it before? He must have been too caught up in the chase.

The scent of wolf—not a natural pack—but a member of his own kind.

He broke into a clearing and stopped short.

The deer lay bloodied on the ground. Its hooves pawed the ground helplessly until the last of its life blood ebbed away, and then the animal fell still.

Just behind, leaning against the thick expanse of a pine tree trunk, stood a naked man. Fresh blood coated his chest and chin. He shared Blake's caramel complexion, dark eyes, and fringe of thick lashes. Long black hair fell down over his naked chest, back, and shoulders. His casual stance—arms folded across his chest, one ankle over the other—was the opposite of Blake's drummed-in military posture.

The man smiled at the wolf. "Hello, Cuz."

Chogan Pallaton.

Blake growled again, lowering his big head, the hackles on his back rising, making his already huge form appear even bigger.

But his cousin showed no fear. Instead, he cocked an eyebrow, one side of his mouth curling in a smirk. "You can't intimidate me,

Blake. I've known you since you were only a couple of years old. And you might be bigger than me, but you know I'm faster."

This was true. Though Chogan was still a big guy, a little over six feet tall with a well-muscled but lean body, he'd beat Blake in a race any day of the week. No wonder he'd managed to hunt down the deer before Blake had even gotten near. He'd simply outrun them both.

Blake growled again. He'd not seen his cousin for several years, and he sure as hell didn't want to be standing here with him now. But he couldn't question his cousin's sudden appearance in wolf form.

Go, he willed his spirit guide. *Leave me now.*

The energy sucked from his body and he tensed, waiting for the pain he knew would follow. The change from wolf to man was almost as painful as the other way around. The fur retracted from his body, leaving smooth brown skin. His ears folded against his head and seemed to melt away. His bones snapped and rearranged themselves.

Naked, he stood before his cousin, experiencing no shame at his nudity. Growing up with a wolf-guide, he'd grown used to being without clothing.

"Chogan," he growled. "What the hell are you doing down this far?"

"I'm here to find you, of course."

"Why would you want to find me?"

"I need your help."

Blake snarled. "I've got no interest in helping you."

"I'm not like you, Blake. I didn't turn my back on my people at the slightest hint of trouble."

"That's because you are the trouble."

Chogan waved a hand dismissively. "Not all the time. Anyway, I needed to find you. I'm hoping you might be able to shed some light on a subject that's got people concerned."

Blake frowned. "Like what?"

"There's rumors of spirit shifters disappearing."

"Why would I know anything about that?" he said with a scowl.

"I don't expect you to, but some of the elders have been urging me to get in touch with you, to see if you might use your connections to find out if anything has been reported."

"I don't work for the police department."

"No. Even better, you work for the government. Those guys know everything."

"Not quite everything," Blake muttered. But he needed to find out what was getting people all stirred up. "So what's going on?"

"One of the shifters who went missing is from the reservation. She went to bed as normal, but when her family woke, she was missing. No one has seen any sign of her and it's not like her. She's dedicated to her family and her community ..."

Blake cringed at his words, his metaphorical hackles rising. He'd left the reservation for a reason; just the memory of the place brought him pain. Perhaps he'd only been young, but he'd thought he had the whole of his life mapped out before him. Then one single event had changed everything, and his cousin had played his part in that happening. He would never forgive him.

"I'll see what I can look into, but I don't want you anywhere near me."

Blake turned on his heel and strode back through the forest, heading back to where he'd left his clothing. He had small bundles of clothes hidden around the forest in case his runs took him too far, but in this case his closest clothing was back where he'd started.

He became aware of his cousin walking along behind him.

Blake drew to a halt and Chogan stopped with him. "What do you think you're doing?"

His cousin cocked his head, his long hair falling down to cover one brown shoulder. "What do you think? I'm coming with you."

Blake strode off, shaking his head. "No way."

Light footsteps followed. "I'm planning on staying around, Cuz. There's something going on, and I plan on hanging out till you agree to help me."

CHAPTER FOUR

AUTUMN FITTED THE key into the lock on her front door and turned it. The apartment door cracked open to a blast of music and the scent of food cooking. A smile tugged her mouth. She was glad to be home.

"Hey, girl!" Her roommate Mia's dark head popped around from the kitchen door. "How did it go?"

Immediately, her thoughts turned to the beautiful giant of a man who'd touched her mouth. She could still feel the heat of his finger against her lip. "How did what go?"

Mia's fine eyebrows arched. "Err, let's see. Could I be talking about this elusive interview you've been unable to speak about all week?"

"Oh, yeah, of course." She gave her head a shake. "It went well. I got the job."

Mia jumped up and down, clapping her hands. "Yay! I knew you would. Now why am I the one celebrating while you're acting all mysterious?"

Though the other woman was three years younger than Autumn's own twenty-seven years, their mothers had been best friends and the two girls had grown up like sisters. After Autumn's mom died, Mia's mother had treated her like her own child and she'd spent numerous nights at their family home when her father had needed to work late.

Autumn didn't need a roommate for the rent. She was even a little embarrassed that she'd not taken the more adult step of living alone, but the truth was she found living alone to be unbearably lonely.

Plus, Mia was like the wife Autumn would never have. Mia loved to cook, where Autumn was capable of burning water. The younger woman was more than happy playing the role of homemaker, but Autumn couldn't think of anything worse. She hoped her friend would find a guy soon. At five-two, with her big dark eyes, tiny nose, and cropped hair, she was more than a catch for any man. Autumn knew Mia wanted a family of her own one day, and part of Autumn dreaded such a thing happening, as it would mean she'd end up alone. However, she'd still be overjoyed if Mia met the right man.

"Sorry, I didn't mean to be. The experience was a little strange, that's all."

She followed Mia into the kitchen. Her roommate opened the fridge and, without even needing to be asked, pulled out a chilled bottle of white wine. Autumn settled herself at the kitchen counter as Mia poured out a couple of good-sized glasses and sat opposite.

"Strange how?"

"There was a man who…"

Mia leaned toward her, her eyes bright. "Who, what?"

She shook her head and looked down into her wineglass. "Who left an impression on me."

"Oh. My. God. He's not going to be your boss, is he?"

Autumn laughed and some of the tension ebbed from her body. She took a sip of the wine, enjoying the crisp taste. "No, nothing like that. Though we will be on the same team. He was just really … intense."

"And sexy?" Mia waggled her eyebrows up and down. "Please say he was sexy."

"He was big and…intense."

"Seriously, Autumn, you need to find yourself some more descriptive words." She leaned even farther forward. "So how big was he?"

Autumn frowned slightly, remembering. "Well over six feet, and buff as well. His biceps were as big as my head."

"Holy cow." Mia grinned. "That's big."

Autumn wanted to tell Mia how it had felt to have his finger press against her mouth, as though his skin had literally burned hers, and she could still sense its presence. She wanted to tell her how she couldn't erase the memory of those almost-black eyes piercing hers. Yet, somehow she couldn't bring herself to discuss those details over a girly chat, feeling as though it would diminish their importance somehow.

Important? I barely said more than a few words to him. How could they have been important?

"Oh, it was nothing," she said dismissively. "Just a cute guy. So what's for dinner? Can I help?"

Mia hopped off the stool, went to the oven, and pulled out a dish of baked pasta. "Nope, you're good. How does Italian sound?"

"Perfect. You know I'd marry you, right?"

Mia dropped the baking dish of steaming pasta onto a mat on the counter. "As much as I love you, honey, I'm afraid you just don't do it for me."

Autumn let out an over-exaggerated sigh. "Shame. Me neither."

Her friend spooned creamy pasta onto both of their plates and sat back down. She lifted her wine glass and clinked it against Autumn's. "To hot guys, right? And not needing to marry our girlfriends."

Autumn laughed. "I'll drink to that!"

THE FOLLOWING MORNING, Autumn entered the government building to find the same security staff waiting behind the dark glass door. She looked around, hopeful to see Blake Wolfcollar, but there was no sign of anyone else.

One of the guards, a man in his late thirties, stood as she walked in. "Ma'am," he said with a nod, handing her a security badge. This time, she noted, there was no *visitor* under her name. It seemed she was now a full-fledged member of staff. "General Dumas said to send you straight down to the labs."

"Down?" She'd assumed she had entered on the bottom floor.

"Yes, minus one." He nodded toward the bank of elevators.

Autumn repeated the paces of the previous day and dropped her belongings into the tray. She walked through the metal detector and waited for her purse and shoes to come trundling through on the roller.

The belt came to a stop, capturing her stuff inside the metal block of the scanner. Autumn frowned and tried to peer in, though the black rubber flaps which hung down over the exit blocked her view.

"Is something wrong?" she asked, straightening to look at one of the guards. She was suddenly filled with an irrational fear that some contraband had been planted in either her suit jacket, which she'd run through the scanner, or her purse.

The guard frowned and stared at the controls, his eyes flicking back up to the screen. He shook his head. "Damn thing's been acting up all morning." He made his way to the start of the belt, reached inside, and fiddled with something. A few seconds later, the belt creaked and juddered and got moving again.

Autumn's belongings appeared through the rubber flaps.

"Sorry about that," the guard said.

Relieved she wasn't going to be in trouble for something she hadn't done, she grabbed her things and slipped her jacket and shoes back on. "No, problem," she told him and headed to the elevator. Inside the mirror-walled box, she noticed what she hadn't before—the minus number on the keypad. Below it was another button that seemed to only allow access with a pad, she assumed, for an authorized fingerprint. She shouldn't be surprised. This was a government facility; she almost expected them to have secret floors.

She hit minus one, the little light behind the silver key illuminating in red. The doors closed and she felt the downward motion of the equipment before coming to a stop.

The doors slid open and she stifled a small cry of surprise. Dumas stood directly on the other side, a mere foot separating them. Just behind his left shoulder stood another man she hadn't seen before. He looked to be in his late twenties or early thirties, though something about his gray eyes—an intelligence—made him appear older. His brown hair was brushed back from strong features, flecks of white at the temples.

The two men weren't the only people waiting for her. Farther back, she saw the broad expanse of Blake Wolfcollar. His eyes rested on her face, his gaze clear and direct. His brown eyes were so dark and deep she felt like she was diving into twin cups of molten hot chocolate.

Her stomach did a little flip.

Behind them stretched a huge glass and chrome laboratory. Several rooms were cornered off. Near the back, she caught sight of a couple of people in white coats flitting from room to room like moths trapped in a lampshade.

Dumas smiled his cool smile and stepped back. "Welcome to your new lab."

She stepped out, her eyes wide. She'd expected a busy, hectic laboratory, but this place was close to deserted. "Shouldn't I have a team working with me?"

"No, Doctor, it's just you."

Strange, but what could she say?

He turned to the men flanking him. "You've met Blake Wolfcollar, of course." His attention moved to the other man. "This is Peter Haverly. He's the head of our research department."

She smiled and stepped forward, offering her hand. Peter Haverly took it, his grip dry and firm. "Good to meet you," she said.

He smiled back, his expression warm, unlike Dumas'. "You too."

Dumas began to stride across the lab. "Please, come with me. I have something I need to show you."

He took her over to a bench lined with several stools. Large silver filing cabinets containing slide samples propped up one wall. Across another wall were a chemical extraction chamber, several centrifuges, and bottles of chemicals. On the bench stood high-tech electron microscopes, the most powerful she'd ever seen, together with electron, scanning tunneling, and atomic force microscopes used to view individual DNA molecules.

The head of research handed her a white lab coat.

Autumn waved it away. "Oh, that's fine. I brought my own, but thank you."

Haverly shook his head. "You need to wear this one. I'm afraid I insist. We wouldn't want any outside material tainting what work has already been done."

She took the coat, and he handed her a pair of micro-thin gloves and a pair of Perspex goggles. She glanced over to check the location of Blake.

The big security man hung in the background, his expression unreadable, his arms folded across his chest, making his big biceps appear even larger. She didn't want to feel like a total nerd in her work clothes, but she couldn't do anything about that, so she slipped on the coat, gloves, and goggles.

Dumas nodded at one of the stools. "Please, sit. I want to show you what you're going to be working with."

She took a seat and Dumas sat next to her. Haverly stood behind them, flanking their shoulders. Dumas pulled one of the big microscopes toward him. From one of the filing cabinets, he took out a tray of glass slides, each slide about two inches in length by an inch in width. He selected one and slid the sample beneath the lens of the microscope. In front of them, a large monitor displayed the image of the genetic fragment.

Autumn peered at the screen, a frown furrowing her forehead. "Is this what I'm supposed to be working on?"

Dumas studied her face. "That's right."

"These genes are clearly human. You must realize I would recognize that immediately."

He lifted a finger to stop her. "Just wait. First you must learn about what we need them to become."

Dumas removed the first slide and replaced it with another. "As you can see, the mutation starts small, an amino acid base pair substitution at position five of the polypeptide chain. The adenine-thymine pair for guanine-cytosine."

Autumn nodded her understanding. She hadn't come across this particular mutation before, but she'd guessed that considering her involvement and the total secrecy surrounding the project, this would be something new.

"Of course," the General continued, "your predecessors have already figured out how to create this mutation, simply by using an expression vector to substitute one base pair for another."

Again, Autumn nodded. What he was explaining was simple genetic engineering.

Haverly interrupted. "However, it's the recombinant protein that is causing us problems."

She was almost surprised to hear his voice. She couldn't help but wonder, considering he was the head of R&D, why Dumas was the one talking her through all of this. She got the impression this project was very much the older man's baby.

"That's right," Dumas said, regaining her attention.

Autumn frowned. "The recombinant DNA isn't producing the correct protein?"

"Yes, it is, but the protein isn't going on to have the same effect that we've seen in the genes of our live subjects."

"Which is?"

Dumas pushed the microscope out of the way and reached across to the computer's keyboard. "This is what happens to the human chromosomes once the mutant protein is released into the living subject's body."

On screen, she recognized the familiar shapes of human chromosomes. Before her eyes, they began to divide, the normal number of forty-six pairs splitting and dividing. Autumn blinked and, almost comically, rubbed her eyes beneath her goggles. Surely she wasn't seeing what she thought? On the computer monitor, strands of DNA replicated, creating whole new chromosomes.

She counted them. "Seventy-eight," she said. "So the same number as ...," she racked her brains, "a dog."

Dumas nodded. "Or in this case, the same number as a wolf."

Was it her imagination or had Blake stiffened at the mention of his namesake?

She suddenly felt as though she'd been plunged into a science fiction movie. "This isn't anything I've seen before."

"I wouldn't have expected you to."

"But this is impossible. How have you done this?"

"We haven't done anything, Doctor. These samples were taken from a specimen. The specimen has the ability to change from one thing to another, and we were able to take samples of its DNA as it did so. Those slides you've just seen are the chromosomes multiplying by themselves. As I said, we've already managed to create the protein we believe responsible for the multiplication, but it's not having the effect we need. That's where you step in."

She knew her mouth gaped, but seemed unable to pull herself into a more professional stance. "A specimen? A *live* specimen?"

Dumas nodded.

"Can I see it?"

"I'm sorry, but that's classified."

Autumn took a breath and sat back as much as the stool would allow her to. They were asking her to manipulate the human genome to effectively become a new species. "You understand this goes against ethical law?"

Dumas' cool blue gaze hardened. "We're outside of the law, Doctor. Did you really think the government wouldn't be working on this sort of thing behind the scenes?"

She turned to take in the rest of the lab and the amount of work that had already been done here. Whoever worked on this previously had known what they were doing. They'd already managed to isolate and manipulate the coding gene, which had greatly reduced the amount of work she'd need to do going forward, though she had no idea how long it would take her to figure this particular puzzle out. If she'd be able to figure it out at all.

She hesitated before speaking. "So who worked on this project before?"

He turned to her. "I'm sorry?"

"Who worked on this before me? They've done an awful lot of work. I'm amazed someone would get this far into a project only to abandon it."

He scowled. "Some people don't respect our need for confidentiality."

"I assume I'd know them. Anyone who could get this far must be someone respected in our field."

"I believe I just mentioned the word *confidentiality*. I think the same thing applies here."

Heat crept into her cheeks. She felt like a school kid who'd been reprimanded by her head teacher. She didn't appreciate being made to feel like that.

Autumn pulled herself up to her full height and pushed back her shoulders, lifting her chin. "And I appreciate your need for secrecy, but if something happened to cause my predecessor to walk out during the middle of their work, I think I'm well within my rights to ask a few questions."

She sensed the other men's eyes upon her and forced herself not to waver. She'd learned long ago that if she let people think of her as some young, blonde, push-around, then that was exactly how they'd treat her. She needed to have more balls than the average guy and not be afraid to show them off. She held Dumas' gaze, wondering if he'd give in and tell her.

Instead, he broke his stare from hers and got to his feet. "Just do your job, Doctor. If I decide to tell you more at a later date, that will be my decision, not yours."

The other two men took after him, Peter Haverly shooting her a small smile of sympathy. Blake also glanced back, but not with sympathy. Instead, he seemed to be studying her, as though he'd not quite made up his mind about her. They followed Dumas as he made his way to the elevator, leaving her alone once more.

The elevator doors closed and her whole body sagged in relief. That had been way more tension than she needed on a first day. She'd not even had any time to get her head around the job they expected her to do. Yes, she'd done plenty of biomolecular engineering, using viruses as vectors in order to implant new DNA into host cells and forcing the cells to accept the DNA as their own, but what was happening here was completely different. If the slide Dumas had shown her were accurate, the chromosomes were replicating in such a way as to create a different species from the one they originally started with. She'd never heard of anything doing something like that before.

Movement in the corner of the room caught her eye and her gaze shifted toward it. A camera swiveled to take her in. She sighed. Of course she would be watched. She didn't know why she'd thought they'd leave her alone with highly classified material. They'd film her every movement.

Before anything else, she needed to figure out exactly what she was working with.

Autumn settled into her seat at the microscope and got to work.

CHAPTER FIVE

BLAKE STOOD IN the elevator, remaining silent in the background. He hoped this new scientist wouldn't be able to achieve what Dumas wanted. Her doing so could mean the end of his kind living in any sort of secrecy. She seemed smart, a sharp light behind her aqua blue eyes that made him wonder if perhaps she might succeed where so many others had failed. And he'd enjoyed watching her try to take on Dumas, though he'd known she'd never win.

Dumas pressed his finger against the sensor pad to take them down to the bottom level. A red beam scanned his print. Something beeped and they began to move.

Only a couple of Dumas' team were entrusted with the ability to make the elevators descend to this level. Blake was one of them.

The three shifters were still kept captive, the woman now back to human form, her arms and legs already almost healed. Blake had managed to convince Dumas to allow one of the medical team in to strap the limbs, allowing them to heal correctly.

Still, he hated that he'd not yet come up with any kind of plan to set them free without blowing his cover. Now that his cousin and some of the others from the reservation had suspicions that the shifters vanishing had to do with the government, he didn't know how much longer he would be able to stay undercover.

Perhaps I should involve Chogan? Maybe he's the one who can help free the other shifters?

But if he did, he would still risk blowing his cover, and his cousin and the rest of the reservation would learn how deeply involved he was in this whole thing. Would his people understand his reasons for being here or would they call him a traitor?

Blake wondered where his cousin was now. Despite Chogan following him through the forest, Blake had managed to lose him as soon as they'd hit the city. Chicago was his territory, a place unfamiliar to his cousin. Would Chogan still be hanging around, or would he have made his way back to the reservation?

Blake's concern for the opinions of the people he'd left behind almost ten years prior wasn't his only worry. If Dumas and his team caught Chogan trying to free the shifters, they would quickly make the connection to back him. His cousin would never be able to get inside the building without his help. How would he even get Chogan into the facility? Security was tight. To get Chogan into the building and rescue the shifters, Blake knew there was a chance people would die.

He pushed his worries for the captive shifters from his head. He couldn't focus on that right now, couldn't allow his concern for a few individuals to distract him from the bigger issues at hand. He needed to be right here, near the lab, just in case this new scientist did what the others had been unable to. If she failed, as her predecessors had, Dumas would be running out of options. Yet he couldn't help feeling like there was something special about Autumn Anderson. When Dumas had been explaining to her about the chromosome number, Blake's wolf guide had trotted up to Autumn, nuzzled its nose against her palm, and placed its big, shaggy head in her lap. Of course, she couldn't have noticed anything, but for some reason she had chosen that moment to turn to him. On some subconscious level, had the young doctor been aware of the spirit in their midst?

The elevator doors slid open. Dumas and Haverly stepped out, Blake following close behind. He stopped short. Several other people waited in the room, facing the glass wall which separated the captive shifters from the people who held them prisoner.

His gut twisted at the sight of Calvin Thorne standing among them. Though technically he and Cal were on the same security team, no love was lost between the two men. Calvin made little secret of the fact he coveted Blake's job as Dumas' head of security.

Blake didn't care about that; the other man was welcome to the job just as soon as Blake put an end to Dumas' interest in shifters. But there was something about the man that didn't sit easy with him. He knew Cal had seen plenty of active duty before coming to work for the department, and he couldn't help but feel the man had gotten a taste for the fight. Though the man was presentable enough, with his well-built body, blond hair, and square jaw, there was something about him that made Blake uneasy. Calvin Thorne was hard. While Blake could act tough when he needed to, Cal didn't need to act. Sometimes, Blake wondered if anything existed behind those cold gray eyes.

But the two men accompanying Cal weren't part of the security team. They were part of medical.

He didn't like this. *Why would security need to oversee medical? And why hadn't he been informed?*

From the expression on Peter Haverly's face, the subtle way the other man's jaw tightened and a muscle twitched directly below his left eye, Blake guessed his comrade hadn't been expecting these new arrivals either.

Haverly narrowed his eyes at Dumas. "What's going on?"

"Doctor Anderson has all the samples she'll need, so we should do something more productive than just have them sitting here. After all, we can't send them back out into the rest of the world." He rubbed his hands together. "A good old-fashioned autopsy. I want to see what happens to their bodies when they change."

Haverly stared at him in horror. "How are you going to do that?"

"Open them up and get them to change into whatever animal they can. I want to watch how their bones alter, how their organs reform while they're changing. I figured we'd need some extra backup, which is why Thorne is here."

Blake could stay quiet no longer. "They're not going to be able to shift if they're dead!"

"I don't want them dead. It's possible to open someone up while they're still alive, still conscious."

Haverly's jaw clenched. "This is unnecessary and barbaric!" he spat through gritted teeth.

He and Blake exchanged a worried look. They couldn't stand by and let this happen.

Dumas rounded on Haverly. "I'm not asking for your permission, Haverly. This is my project and I'll decide what happens."

Calvin Thorne regarded the exchange, a cold humor barely hidden beneath the restrained surface of his expression.

The boy sat in the chair, his head down. Silent tears ran down his face, his hands still shackled to the armrests, rendering him unable to wipe the moisture away. A desperate urge overtook Blake, a need to go and reassure him, offer him some kind of comfort. But if he went in there, the boy would recognize what he was and there was a chance of his cover being blown. He shuddered to think what Dumas would do if he discovered his head of security was one of those he seemed to both despise and adore.

The head of the project nodded at Calvin. The two medics waited with small, slender boxes which Blake felt certain held hypodermic needles containing some kind of sedative.

"Take the man," Dumas instructed, nodding toward the chambers.

Without a word, the men took the passageway to the right, which lead behind the glass screen and to the back of the holding cells. Cal folded his arms across his chest, the expression on his face never changing.

Blake watched through the one-way glass, his fists clenched. He was torn, desperately wanting to shift and rip these people apart, but knowing he couldn't.

The captive man turned as if he'd heard something, and the next moment a hidden door in the metal wall at the back of his chamber opened. The men in white coats entered the room, syringes in hand. The man's eyes widened. He struggled, yanking his bound feet and hands. The cuffs didn't budge.

He turned to the front and locked eyes with Blake, though Blake knew he couldn't see him through the glass. The eye contact must be coincidence, the man had no way of knowing another shifter stood on the other side.

The man's eyes flared a golden yellow.

Blake knew what that meant. He launched forward, slamming his hand down on the button which allowed him to speak into the chamber. "Get out! He's shifting!"

The world seemed to pause as the man's whole body tensed. His hair withered and vanished and what appeared to be quills spiked from his body. He roared in pain as they stabbed through his skin. His body yanked one way and the next, then the quills unfurled.

Feathers, Blake realized.

The man's face changed, his nose and mouth molding together and elongating, covered in a hard, brittle material. His whole body shrank, his arms and legs slipping from both his clothing and the ties which bound him. His clothes fell in a pile on the floor.

The men took a couple of steps away, their backs against the wall, looking on with a mixture of amazement and horror. Where only moments before a man sat, now a huge eagle stood perched on the chair. The bird was larger than any of them had ever seen before, easily four times that of a regular eagle.

The bird opened its beak and screeched.

It spread its massive wings, spanning almost half the room.

Dumas seemed to remember himself. He pushed Blake out of the way to get to the microphone. "Sedate it!" he yelled at the doctors.

They exchanged a glance and both lunged forward. The bird flapped its wings and lifted into the air. The men tried to grab hold of it, but it fought back. Huge talons swiped at the men, opening a huge gash in one of their cheeks, almost taking out an eye. The man cried out and fell back, his hand clutched to his face, blood pouring from between his fingers. His colleague took one look at the blood and dropped to the ground. The bird dived at him with another screech, two-inch talons open to grab him.

Dumas rounded on Blake and Cal. "Well? What are you waiting for? Get in there!"

With uncertainty, Cal looked between the scene behind the glass and Dumas. It wasn't often Blake had seen him rattled, but right now the other man didn't seem to know what to make of what was happening. *It's the first time he's witnessed a shift,* Blake realized. Nevertheless, Calvin's hand automatically went to the weapon holstered on his hip.

"What are you playing at?" Dumas yelled, clearly frustrated with their lack of response. "You want to hold each other's hands?"

Still, Blake hesitated. He knew the other shifter would be able to sense what he was, would feel the extra heat radiating from his body. He didn't want to go into the chambers with the other shifter. If the man blew his cover, this whole thing would be over.

Dumas glared at him and then reached inside his jacket pocket and pulled out a small pistol. "Damn it. If you want something done—"

Blake put out a hand to stop him. "I'm on it."

Calvin stood there, confusion written on his face.

At a jog, Blake followed the same route the two men in white coats had taken, running down a narrow corridor which led to the back of the holding cells. He entered the chamber through the same metal door as the two guys from medical.

The bird sat on top of one of the men. The man cowered, crying and gibbering, his arms held over his face for protection. The bird's bright, black eyes focused on Blake as he entered the room.

He put his hands up in defense. "I'm not going to hurt you."

The bird opened its beak, revealing a soft, pink palate, and screeched again. The sound echoed around the small space, enough to make Blake's ears hurt.

"You need to shift back," he hissed. "They'll shoot you if you don't."

It spread its wings and flapped, causing a gust of air to blow against Blake's face and body. One of the doctors cried out in alarm.

Blake spread out his hands, a pleading gesture. "Please. Just shift back. If you don't, they'll kill you. There's no getting out of this place like this." He stared into the bird's eyes, desperately trying to communicate what was in his heart, in his head.

I'll help you. As soon as I can.

The bird ducked its smooth round head, its wings still outstretched. It went rigid, shudders racking its body. The feathers retracted, pulling back beneath the skin to leave pink, smooth skin. The wings first reduced in size, and then grew bigger, fingers sprouting where long wing-feathers had just been. The beak shrank, molding back into the face to create a nose and mouth. The bird's eyes burned yellow and then returned to the man's normal color.

Now back in human form, the naked man crouched on top of the doctor.

Blake didn't care too greatly for the injuries of the doctors who'd been intent on hurting the shifter, but he didn't want the shifter to be harmed. He approached with caution, his hands held out. "Everything is going to be all right. We'll work this out."

The man's eyes narrowed. "How can you say that?"

"I'll do everything I can."

"Get word to my family—"

Dumas' voice blared into the room. "Don't talk to it, Blake. Just get them out of there!"

Blake grabbed the injured doctors, and, using his huge strength, hoisted them out of the room, through the small corridor and back into the surveillance unit where Dumas waited. The men continued to cry, clutching their injuries. Blood stained their white coats like a butcher's apron.

"God-damned freaks," Dumas muttered. He rounded on Blake. "What the hell was that all about?"

Blake glared back. "What?"

"All the 'We'll work this out' bullshit."

"I was trying to talk him down, General. You almost had two dead men, and not to mention the potential mutilation of an innocent man." His eyes flicked to Cal. "And at least I did something."

Calvin's shoulders squared and he glared back at Blake.

Dumas' face grew red. "I suggest you take some time to get control of yourself, Sergeant."

I'm more in control of myself than I hope you'll ever find out.

He could feel the desire to shift burning at his nerve endings. He wanted nothing more than to call his wolf to him and show Dumas exactly what he was dealing with. But from behind Dumas' shoulder, Haverly stared at Blake in warning.

A groan came from the floor where Blake had dropped the two guys from medical.

Dumas looked toward the noise and wrinkled his nose. "And Christ, someone sort out a medic for these two. They're bleeding all over my floor." He shook his head in disgust and stormed from the room. Cal hurried after him.

Haverly opened his mouth to speak, but a glare from Blake shot him down. "Don't say a word," he snapped. "You wouldn't have done any different."

The other man stared at him. "I think Dumas is right. Go and cool down."

BLAKE TROTTED DOWN the steps of the building and stepped out onto the street. He walked quickly, his head down, hands stuffed into his pockets. His emotions were in turmoil. What would have happened if the man had been less able to control his ability to shift? What if he'd been taken away and laid out on a surgical table somewhere and cut open purely to placate Dumas' sick interests? Would he have been able to stand by then?

He suddenly became aware of someone behind him. He spun around to find the increasingly familiar form of his cousin standing in the street. The other man's long hair was tied back, and he wore an easy grin.

Blake didn't return the smile. "What the hell are you doing here?"

"I think I already told you that."

"You shouldn't even know where I work."

He cocked an eyebrow. "I followed you. You don't exactly blend in."

It was true. At six-feet-four, with his brown skin, almost-black eyes, and well-muscled torso, he wasn't one to fit into a crowd. But then, neither was his cousin.

He wanted to keep Chogan as far away from the research facility as possible.

"Fine, walk with me."

The two men set off down the street, side by side.

"So have you had any chance to look into what I asked?" said Chogan.

Blake shook his head. "I don't know what you think it is I'm supposed to look for. I'm hardly going to be informed if they're capturing shifters and using them for God-knows-what."

His cousin jerked his head back the way they'd come. "What is it they do in there, anyway?"

"Research and development."

"Of what?"

"I don't know," Blake said, suddenly exasperated. "Whatever needs to be researched and developed. I'm hardly hired for my mind, am I?"

"Don't give me that bullshit. You're smart. You always were."

Blake stopped walking. "Listen. I'll keep my ear to the ground and see if I can find anything out. But I'm not making any promises. I do what I'm told in that place, and that's it."

"Your problem is that you have more loyalty to the people who pay your wages than you do those who raised you."

"You have no idea what you're talking about!"

"No? Then why haven't you even been back to visit in almost ten years?"

"You, of all people, should understand the reason for that."

"Don't punish everyone else for what happened, Blake. None of that was their fault."

Blake growled in frustration. "No, it was yours." And with that, he stormed off, leaving Chogan standing on the sidewalk.

CHAPTER SIX

MIA HENDERSON LIFTED her coffee cup and took a sip of her now lukewarm coffee. She checked her watch again and tapped her foot in a thrumming beat on the floor beneath her table.

Did I get the time wrong? Or perhaps the place?

Her eyes travelled over the people sharing the cafe with her—a man and a woman wearing business suits, a small group of student-types laughing with their heads together, a solitary woman writing on a laptop. None of these people fitted the profile of a worried, frightened couple.

She sighed and reached into her bag to pull out the paperwork containing the profile of the missing boy.

Toby West, fifteen years old. Missing for nine days now. She stared down at the boy's photograph. He stared sullenly into the camera, his too-long dark hair falling into his face. Across the chest of his t-shirt was scrawled the name of a band Mia had never heard of, but one the boy's friends said he idolized. He may have been wearing the same shirt the night he went missing.

A pang of loss and what...regret?...clutched her heart. Marcus might have looked like this at some point if he were still alive, something Mia was starting to feel like she'd never know for sure. Her twin brother had vanished one day on the way home from school. Normally, they walked together, but Mia had an afterschool music class that day, so Marcus had gone home alone. Except he'd never reached his destination.

Other than losing your own child, was there anything worse than losing your twin? She literally felt as though half of her was missing. No wonder she'd set up this charity as soon as she'd gotten out of school. It had taken a lot of hard work and she'd needed to cut through a lot of red tape, but she'd been determined to see it through. She wanted nothing else from her life except, perhaps, to have a family of her own one day, a way to fill the aching hole in her heart that had appeared the same day her brother vanished.

The bell on the cafe door dinged and Mia glanced up. A beaten-down, middle-aged couple pushed their way into the cafe, the man's arm around the woman's waist, the woman's eyes darting around the room.

Mia straightened in her seat and tried to make eye contact with the new arrivals, a sympathetic smile on her face. The woman caught her eye and glanced away uncertainly, checking the rest of the room before coming back to her. She nudged her husband and nodded in Mia's direction. They swerved between the chairs and tables to come to stand opposite. The woman, her blonde hair cut in a bob around her face, her blue eyes rimmed red, offered her an apologetic smile.

"I'm sorry we're late," she said. "My husband wasn't keen on coming to you for help. He needed a little...persuading."

Mia gestured to the seats opposite for them to sit down. "I completely understand, Mrs. West."

"Call me Dana, please," said the woman as she took a seat. "And this is my husband, Robert."

The husband didn't make eye contact with her, but instead stared at the table, his hands clutched in his lap. Right away, Mia could see where their son had inherited his dark looks. Toby was the spitting image of his father.

She caught Dana staring at her.

"I'm sorry." Dana gestured to her own features. "I had thought you'd be...older."

Mia smiled. "Don't worry. You're not the first person to say that. I got involved with charity work right out of school. I can promise you I know what I'm doing, Mr. and Mrs. West."

Instead of following the majority of her friends to college, Mia had left high school to spend her days volunteering at another missing person's charity, and her evenings and weekends working the front desk of a hotel. She'd saved every penny and two years later had used the money to start up her own charity, Missing Lives.

"Oh, I wasn't trying to imply—"

Mia cut her off. "It's fine, honest. Now, I've got the background the police compiled about your son, but what I really want to find out is about the real boy. Not just the front he might put on to everyone else, perhaps even including yourselves. And please, don't worry about being unsure about all of this. Often people feel like they're taking charity by coming to us, but that's the whole point in our existence. We use all of the money donated to us to pool into finding missing people, to putting in extra resources, hiring PI's perhaps, when the police think their leads have cooled."

She saw the expression on Dana's face. "I'm not saying their leads *have* cooled of course," she hastily added.

Dana's forehead crumpled. "They don't have any leads. It's like someone snatched him off the face of the earth!"

Robert took his wife's hand, finally lifting his eyes to Mia. "The police say he probably ran away. He's been having some problems at school, getting into fights and stuff. The police have got him painted up as some kind of young thug, but he's not like that."

Many of the cases Mia took on were similar to Toby's. She was perfectly aware of the correlation between her searching for all these lost boys and her own desire to find her missing twin brother. Perhaps she hoped one day she would be able to unearth the secret about what happened to him, stumble across some kind of clue that could bring her continual searching to an end.

"No, he's not," Dana interrupted. "Our son, he's...well...different."

Robert shot his wife a glare.

"Of course," Mia said, trying to empathize. "All children are different, all their own individuals—"

"That wasn't what I meant," Dana said.

"Dana..."

It was impossible not to recognize the warning tone in the husband's voice.

What's going on here?

Dana shrugged off her husband's warning and leaned over the table, closing the gap between herself and Mia. She lowered her voice as if she was worried someone might overhear them. "We know our son, Ms. Henderson. Perhaps more so than most parents know their teenage boys. Like we said, he's different from other boys, different in a way I'm not even sure how to explain. We think those differences may have something to do with the reason he's gone missing."

"Okay," Mia said slowly. "You're going to need to give me a little more to work on than just 'different.'"

Dana clenched her jaw and nodded.

The other woman's strength amazed Mia. She understood how it felt when someone you loved went missing, to have so many questions, questions you would probably never learn the answers to. She didn't know how Dana was holding herself together.

Robert sighed and leaned across the table, matching his wife's stance. He began to speak, obviously giving in to his wife's way of thinking. "Toby has a way of zoning out sometimes, like he's not even in the room with you or his head is somewhere else. He's got a way of seeing things that are about to happen. And I don't mean predicting world events or anything like that, but he'll say things like 'A cab is about to come around the corner,' and the next moment, that's exactly what happens."

He seemed to run out of steam, and his wife nudged him in the ribs. "Go on, tell her the rest."

"It's going to sound crazy," he said.

Mia offered a reassuring smile. "I can handle crazy."

The man's dark eyes flicked down to the table and he reached out to fiddle with the little pot of sugars and sweeteners. "He vanishes from his room at night. He'll go to bed and we'll go in to check on him and he'll be gone. The window is normally left open."

"It's pretty normal for a teenage boy to sneak out at night."

"We live on the fifth floor of an apartment block in the city," Dana said.

"Oh!" Mia blinked in surprise. "He's sneaking out by the front door, then?"

"Impossible," Robert said. "We've gone to extra measures to deadlock the door and keep the key on us, so we know he's not getting out that way."

"Have you asked him about all this?"

Dana nodded. "He always told us he couldn't remember. We even took him to a psychiatrist at one stage, but the doctor said the only explanation he could give was that Toby's dream world and waking world were spilling into one. He was basically sleepwalking."

"Isn't that a possibility?"

"I'd say perhaps, but that's not all."

"No?"

"Sometimes, when we've gone to wake him up the next morning, we find mud and twigs or leaves on his bed sheets or the window sill and rug."

Robert spoke again, quietly. "And sometimes the mud is on his hands and feet as well, as if he's been running around in it."

Mia frowned. "But your son remembers none of this?"

Robert and Dana shook their heads in unison.

"What do the police say?"

Dana's restraint finally broke down. Her voice cracked and she stifled a sob with the back of her clenched fist pressed against her mouth. "I'm sorry."

Mia smiled reassuringly and reached across the table to place her hand over Dana's. "You don't need to be."

The older woman nodded and continued. "They only know Toby is a sleepwalker and we've taken him to a doctor about it. We didn't dare mention any of the other stuff in case they thought we were nuts as well."

Mia understood where they were coming from. So often, she'd discovered parents worried about divulging information to the police, terrified they would end up looking like the perpetrators of whatever crime had removed their child from their lives.

"Leave this with me," she told them. "You've given me a couple of things I can get started on. If you hear anything else, call me as soon as you can."

MIA WALKED AWAY confused and disbelieving. Surely these parents weren't trying to say what she thought? In fact, she wasn't even sure what it was they *were* trying to say!

At least she felt like she might have something new to go on. Her first port of call was to get a map of the city, pinpoint the family's apartment, and mark out each of the parks nearby. If the boy had somehow been getting out of the apartment in the middle of the night—be it consciously or subconsciously—then it sounded like he was heading to wooded areas when he did so. When Toby went missing from his bedroom, there was a good chance he might have been on one of his excursions. Perhaps someone saw him or someone who looked suspicious.

The shrill of her phone ringing came from her purse. She delved around to fish out her smartphone and swiped the screen to answer.

"Mia Henderson," she chirped.

The voice on the other end was muffled, but she recognized it instantly. "Mia, you need to come back to the office." She heard her assistant sniff, her breath hitching. She was trying not to cry.

"What is it, Tina? What's wrong?"

"I've just opened a letter from the State Department. They're cutting our funding."

"*What?* Did they say why?"

"Only that the tough financial climate has meant they've needed to make some difficult cuts. I guess we were one of them."

Mia tried to stem the worry bubbling up inside her. "I'm on West Washington Street. I'll be with you in fifteen minutes."

CHAPTER SEVEN

BLAKE WATCHED AUTUMN leave the building, her smart suit jacket pulled up around her ears in protection against the cool evening. As she walked, she reached behind her head and unclipped her hair. The spiral blonde curls fell around her neck and shoulders, and she ran a hand through them to shake them loose.

How would those curls feel beneath his palm? Soft like silk?

He shook the thought from his head. This was business. He couldn't let himself think in such a way.

Blake didn't feel the cold, one of the benefits of his metabolism running at an abnormally high rate. The other advantage was his ability to stay in shape, without an ounce of fat on his body. Despite this, he didn't take his physique for granted. Though he never stepped into a gym, he made sure his apartment had enough equipment to allow him to work his body to the point of exhaustion. He didn't work out for vanity, but for practical reasons. He hated the possibility of getting into a situation only to be beaten simply because he wasn't strong enough.

Out of habit, to fit in with the rest of society, Blake wore a black leather jacket, though he had no need for the item. His skin burned hot beneath the insulated material and he knew he'd be more comfortable if he were able to strip off both his jacket and t-shirt and walk bare-chested in the cool evening air. Instead, he turned up the collar, a mimic of Autumn's actions, and broke into a jog after her.

"Doctor Anderson," he called gently. "Wait up."

She turned as he caught up with her. "Oh!" She clutched a hand to her chest. "You startled me."

"Sorry, I didn't mean to."

She gave him an expectant half-smile, a slight worry in her eyes, probably at being on a street alone with a man twice her size.

"I wondered how your first day went."

Autumn arched an eyebrow. "Are you sure I'm allowed to talk about it?"

She surprised a laugh from him. "To me, you are."

"Good to know." She smiled and stuffed her hands into her pockets. "I can't exactly say it went well, but it's early days yet."

"Do you think you'll be able to complete what's been asked of you?"

"You're not going to go back and report to the boss, are you?"

He laughed again and she smiled at the sound. "No, I promise."

Autumn started to walk once more, and he matched her pace. "What he's asking has never been done before," she said. "Plus, the lack of information I have on the subject matter doesn't help." She turned to face him, her eyes narrowed slightly. "You know where the samples came from, don't you? You know what this … species is?"

Blake hesitated, considering his answer. He didn't want to give her any information to help her; the last thing he wanted was for her to succeed at her job. That didn't mean he couldn't give her information which might send her down the wrong track.

He opened his mouth and the words wouldn't come out. He couldn't lie to her. "It's classified," he finished lamely.

She rolled her eyes. "What a surprise. I guess I'll have to do my time before anyone will trust me enough to tell me what's really going on."

"What do you think is going on?"

"Honestly?" She looked to him for confirmation and he nodded. "I wouldn't be surprised if the samples come from some kind of alien species."

The thought of them being aliens made him laugh again.

She frowned, though the corners of her mouth twitched. "What's so funny? You don't think there's a chance of another life form existing in the universe somewhere?"

He grew serious. "Are you asking me if I believe in the paranormal, Doctor Anderson?"

"My name is Autumn, and, yes, I guess I am."

"Then, the answer is absolutely. But surely, as a scientist, the paranormal is the last thing you should believe in."

"I believe that almost everything we now put down to science was once considered to be paranormal."

He studied her face. *Smart, beautiful, and open-minded.* There must be something wrong with this woman. Across the foot of space separating them, the warmth of her skin radiated toward him and he could smell her shampoo and the faint residue of perfume she must have applied that morning.

She must have caught the way he was looking at her, because she slowed to a stop. "What?"

In his head, his wolf growled a warning.

He couldn't allow himself to get caught up in a woman, especially not this one. He forced himself to step away, to straighten his shoulders, and harden his jaw. "A scientist who believes in fairy tales doesn't seem like a very good scientist to me."

Her eyes widened in surprise at his comment. "Is that right? And that's coming from a guy who uses his muscles as his career."

"Is that what you think? I'm no more than Dumas' muscle?"

"Aren't you essentially a pumped-up security guard?"

He held her gaze and her cheeks flushed deeper. "I am so much more than that."

He turned and walked away, leaving her standing on the street. He felt her eyes bore into his back as he left.

AUTUMN WATCHED THE infuriating man storm down the street. What the hell had gotten into him? One minute they'd been having a perfectly normal, interesting conversation, and the next he'd almost turned on her. And the way he looked at her, as though pinning her with his eyes. Had she ever come across someone who was so damn intense?

She regretted what she'd said about him being a piece of muscle. Perhaps she'd reacted unfairly, but he'd touched on a nerve. She's spent her whole career being judged, first for her appearance and secondly for her youth. Men in the late stages of their careers regarded her with both resentment and disbelief as she managed to achieve breakthroughs in their field that had left them stumped. She wished she understood the reason for being so good at what she did, but she was simply given a problem and could see the answer. There were plenty of times in her life where she'd wished she didn't have her talent, or perhaps that she was older and the opposite sex. When she'd been at school, she'd been skipped ahead several years, so all of her peers either looked down their noses at her, or else thought she was a little freak. Plus, she'd blossomed into her looks. As a teenager, she'd been tall and skinny with a halo of frizz-filled hair. Now, she'd learned how to appreciate and dress for her slender, tall frame, and had discovered the miracle of frizz-fighting hair products. But despite all this, she had her job hanging over her and there weren't many men who found science sexy.

Yet now, Blake Wolfcollar had managed to imprint himself upon both her skin and mind. How could she want to hit someone while simultaneously wondering what he looked like with his shirt off?

She exhaled a slow, measured breath. What she needed now was a long, hot bath so she could turn her latest project over in her head, and that didn't mean including Blake in her thoughts. She was being paid a large sum of money to do a job, and she needed to concentrate on that.

A sudden urge to speak to her father washed over her, despite the two of them having a bit of an awkward relationship. He felt responsible for her mother's death, though there was no way he could have either predicted or prevented it.

Anytime she had a puzzle involving science, she wanted to run it by him. Not being able to talk about this particular project was going to be beyond frustrating. Plus, she wondered if they couldn't talk about her work, would they have anything to talk about at all.

She sighed. She wished she was able to talk to him about normal things fathers were interested in—baseball results, a latest DIY project, even politics. But he was so involved in whichever project he was currently working on he'd often forget to even eat, never mind take any interest in the world happening outside of the lab, including his own daughter.

Still, weeks had passed since she'd last seen him, and the sudden spat with Blake Wolfcollar had left her with a deep-seated need to be around the familiar.

She lifted a hand to flag down a cab.

AUTUMN PAID THE driver and climbed from the cab. Paint peeled from the front door of what had once been an immaculate house. Thick grime coated the outsides of the windows and weeds sprouted between the steps leading up to the residence.

Professor John Anderson still lived in the family home where Autumn had grown up. The house was a huge, five-bedroom townhouse on the North Side, with several living rooms and a huge kitchen. Her father barely used much of the house, keeping the rooms shut off, with dust cloths covering the furniture. In the unused rooms, he kept the blinds closed, both to keep the sun off precious furnishings and pictures, and also to keep prying eyes out. The result was a house that looked like no one had lived in it for years. The only rooms Professor Anderson kept in use were the kitchen, the bedroom he'd shared with his wife until her death, the en-suite bathroom, and the basement.

The basement was where her father spent most of his time. Years ago, when Autumn had been small, he'd had the space converted into his own private laboratory.

Autumn rang the bell, only to discover no sound emitted from the device. She rapped on the front door with her knuckles and waited. No movement came from inside. She reached into her purse. She still had a key, but didn't like to use it. This place didn't feel like her home anymore. She knew he'd be in. He never went anywhere except for the few occasions he was called outside of the city for work. Now that he'd retired, those occasions had grown less and less.

Giving up waiting, Autumn let herself in. A pile of mail teetered and spilled across the hall as she pushed open the front door. She bent and scooped most of the letters up, dumping them on the hall console.

"Dad?"

No response.

Autumn sighed. She knew where he'd be.

Down the hall, a door led beneath the stairs.

She descended the brightly lit stairs into the cellar to find her father at a workbench, bent over his equipment. He hadn't even noticed her arrival, and she took a moment to study him, checking if anything about him had changed in the past few weeks, if there was anything she should be more concerned about than usual.

She had gotten her long limbs and height from him, though he wore it in a gangly way, so he often didn't appear to have control of his own body. She'd also inherited his blonde curls, though they'd long since fled her father's pate. His hairline was less receding and more receded, leaving a pink, naked scalp.

Autumn audibly cleared her throat.

He looked up from his work, peering at her from over his safety goggles, a pipette of clear fluid held poised in one hand. "Autumn? What are you doing here?"

She risked a smile. "Hi, Dad. I got a new job."

"Another one? What was wrong with the last one?"

"Nothing was wrong with it, Dad. The contract ended."

He looked back down at his work and dropped fluid from the pipette onto a slide. "Oh, right."

"So don't you want to know what the new job is?"

He shrugged and leaned over the microscope to inspect what he was working on. "Sure."

"I'm working for the government. I can't say much more than that, but it could be interesting. Really interesting."

She waited for a response, but none came. Instead, he switched the slides beneath the scope.

"Dad?" she prompted.

"I'm sorry, was there something you actually wanted, Autumn?"

"Um, no. Just to visit with my dad."

"Well, you can see I'm kind of busy here, sweetheart. So if you don't mind ...?"

"Oh, right."

Hot tears burned behind her eyes, but she refused to let him see them. Why did she think things would be any different? He was always busy. Even when she'd been a child and had lost her mother, he'd been busy. In fact, after her mom had died, he'd thrown himself into his work rather than face up to the fact that she'd gone. He seemed to have forgotten that his daughter hadn't died at the same time as his wife.

Autumn turned and ran from the house, the back of her knuckles pressed against her mouth. She ran out onto the street and straight into someone. The person caught her by the wrists, but she shook them off.

"Hey, it's okay!" A male voice spoke. "You ran into me."

She put out a hand and pushed past the man, barely glancing at him. "I'm sorry..."

"Wait up a minute." Footsteps ran along beside her, and she picked up her pace. "Hey, wait!"

She spun around. "Why should I?" Her temper flared, taking her hurt out on him rather than the person actually responsible for her mood.

"You seem upset."

"Why should you care?" she shot back.

"I don't like to see someone upset."

"You're a stranger."

His voice softened. "Yeah, and I'm guessing it isn't a stranger who's made you cry."

"I'm not crying—" But, with dismay, she realized her cheeks were damp. The anger burned out of her and her shoulders slumped. For the first time, she took in the sight of the concerned stranger. A man with long dark hair tied back, over six feet tall, broad shoulders, high cheekbones and dark eyes. A flutter of recognition appeared inside her, but she couldn't place it.

"Man trouble?" he asked, a hint of a smile playing on his lips.

She couldn't help smile back, and sniffed. "I guess you could say that."

"Well, I'd also say he's a fool."

She sniffed again. "You got that right."

The man held out his hand. "I'm Chogan Pallaton. I just got into town."

She reached out and shook it. His skin was warm. Too warm. "I'm Autumn. Please don't think I'm being rude, but I'm not going to offer to show you around if that's what you're after. I've had a really long day ..."

He held up both hands in defense, his dark eyes lighting with amusement. "Hey, I wouldn't dream of imposing. Another time, perhaps?"

"Yeah." She glanced at him, suddenly shy. "Perhaps."

He gave her a nod and stuffed his hands into his pockets. He ducked his head as he walked away, then threw a glance back over his shoulder, smiling again as Autumn stood watching him.

Why did she feel like she knew him from somewhere?

CHAPTER EIGHT

AUTUMN OPENED THE front door of her apartment and paused. Something was wrong. The usual blare of music and smell of cooking didn't greet her. The apartment was in silence. Had Mia gone out without letting her know she wouldn't be home? That wasn't like her. They normally looked out for one another. But no, she realized, the place wasn't in total silence. A muffled sobbing came from deeper within the building.

Alarm spiked through her. "Mia?"

She rushed to her roommate's bedroom to find the door closed. The crying was definitely coming from inside the room. She lifted her hand and gently knocked before cracking open the door. The cries grew louder. Mia had the drapes drawn and the light was off, so Autumn barely made out her small form curled in on itself on her bed.

"Mia? What's wrong?" Her own problems forgotten, she rushed to her friend's side. She took a seat on the edge of the bed, one hand rubbing Mia's back.

Mia lifted her head from her pillow. In the light from the hallway, Autumn noted her face was puffy from crying, her eyes red-rimmed, and her skin blotchy. "They cut the budget for Missing Lives for next year."

"What? Who has?"

"The government. If I don't find the money, I'll have to shut down."

"That's crazy. How much did they cut it by?"

"Everything. They've pulled the whole lot."

"Are they able to do that?"

"They're the government; they can do whatever they want." She buried her head in her hands. "I'm going to have to let Tina go, and I've just taken on a new case. I can't believe I'm going to let the parents down like this, with everything they're already going through."

"I'm sure they'll understand." She paused. "Who is the new case?"

"A boy—Toby West. He's been missing for nine days now."

Autumn reached out and covered Mia's hand with her own, squeezed it, hoping to offer some kind of comfort. She understood Mia's reason for tending to take on similar cases—teenage boys, often suspected runaways with troubled backgrounds.

"Listen to me. I have money sitting in my account, not doing anything. I'll make a good-sized donation, enough to keep you going for a few months. Perhaps then you'll be able to figure out something else." She smiled. "Maybe we could organize a fundraiser event. There's bound to be other people who know what an amazing job you do and who will be willing to help."

Mia lifted her eyes. It pained Autumn to see their dark pools swimming in tears. "I can't expect you to do that."

"Mia, honey, you're my best friend and the closest thing I have to real family. I know how important Missing Lives is to you. It's your whole life and you've helped so many people. I'm not going to let you go under when I have money that can help you. I mean, what else am I going to do with it?"

What she said was true. She never took a vacation, rarely dated. Her wardrobe consisted of smart but inexpensive suits for work, and then she lived in jeans and sneakers on the weekend. She didn't even have a gym membership, preferring to run the streets of the city plugged into her iPod instead.

"Really? Are you sure?" Mia's chin wobbled and fresh tears sprang to her eyes.

"I wouldn't say something if I didn't mean it." Autumn laughed. "Now stop crying or you're going to make me cry too."

Mia sat up and threw her arms around Autumn's neck in a tight squeeze. "Oh my God. Thank you so much. You're the best friend a girl could have. And I'll pay you back, I swear I will."

"I don't want paying back. It's a donation, not a loan."

THE NEXT MORNING, back in the facility, Autumn had seen no sign of Blake, and she found her heart beat too hard in her chest at the prospect of bumping into him again. She wondered how he'd act when their paths did eventually cross, as they surely would. Would he be cool with her or ignore her completely? Why was this even bothering her so much?

She sat down at the equipment, running back over the slides she'd been working on. Even though much of the work had already been completed by her predecessors, she'd decided to start from scratch by replicating the original mutation. She couldn't trust that things had been done right the first time.

A number of cups of coffee and several hours later, she'd achieved the original mutation, a single base pair amino acid substitution at position five of the polypeptide chain. But the expression of the gene mutation into whole chromosomes replicating simply wasn't happening.

It's early days yet, she reminded herself. *Far too soon to start panicking.*

The ping of the elevator doors opening caught her attention. She turned to see Peter Haverly emerge from the elevator. He donned a white coat and headed over to her. "Hey, how's our newest recruit doing?"

Autumn pulled off her protective glasses and dropped them on the counter. "Slow, though I hope I'm making some progress."

He offered her a smile. "I'm sure you are. Any chance you can run me through what you've done so far?"

His interest confused her. Surely they couldn't expect her to have achieved something already? This could take weeks, if not months. *If*, in fact, she managed to do what they wanted at all. But what could she say? While he might not be her direct boss, he was certainly her superior.

She picked her glasses back up and slid them onto her face. "Sure. I was just about to apply a catalyst to the recombinant DNA. I'm hoping we might see some of the changes we've seen in the original samples."

He pulled up a stool beside her. "Sounds good."

Autumn slid a new slide containing the sample she'd created beneath the electron microscope and locked it into place. Immediately, the strands appeared on the computer screen—like fat X-shaped sausages—clearly made out on the powerful equipment. She took out a pipette and added a drop of clear fluid chemical. She reached in with another, much thinner slide to drop on top of the DNA in order to increase the focus. As she reached in, she pressed too hard and the small sliver of glass snapped, one piece embedding into the fleshy pad of her finger.

"Shit!" She pulled her hand back, careful not to disturb the already primed slide, but before she got clear, a single drop of blood fell onto the sample.

"Oh crap," she swore. "I'm so sorry. I guess I'll need to start again."

Damn it. Why did things like that happen when someone else was watching? She reached out to remove the ruined slide, but a hand caught her by the arm, Haverly's grip hard, stronger than she'd given him credit for.

"Wait!"

She looked in surprise from the man's hand on her arm to his wide-eyed, suddenly pale face which was locked on the monitor screen.

"Look." His voice was breathy, and slowly he dropped his hold on her arm.

Autumn turned to the monitor, a frown creasing her forehead. Then she caught sight of what was happening on screen and gave a gasp.

"I can't believe it."

On the computer, the chromosomes began to separate, creating a different sequence and number, one that might be a different species all together.

"How is that even possible?" she asked, her voice hushed.

He caught hold of her hand once more and lifted it up. Blood ran from the tip, drops spattering the floor.

"Get another slide." His words weren't a request.

She looked at him and then nodded, realizing that whatever had happened needed to be replicated immediately or they might lose the answer to the puzzle she'd been paid to solve.

Quickly, Autumn replicated the experiment, using the sample of recombinant human DNA she'd created herself. On screen, the slide showed a regular number of chromosomes for human DNA. "Now what?" she asked.

"Your blood. You need to add your blood."

With her heart in her throat, she held her finger over the slide, squeezing her finger with her other hand to force a drop of her blood onto the slide.

The moment her blood hit, the chromosomes began to split and reform.

"Oh. My. God."

Haverly leapt to his feet and ran to each corner, flicking something on the security cameras.

"What are you doing?"

"General Dumas can't know about this. Your life is in danger."

The excitement she'd been experiencing flipped to alarm. She jumped up. "What?"

"We don't have long. Security is going to notice the cameras are out soon enough and come to find out what's wrong.

He pulled the slides from beneath the microscope. "We need to destroy these, not that it's going to make much difference. Your work's been recorded since you started and as soon as Dumas reviews the recordings, he's going to see what's happened and come after you."

"Come after me? Why would he do that?"

"Because you're the answer, Doctor Anderson. Your blood is the key to turning regular humans into shifters."

That word again. "Into *what*?!"

"I can't explain now. I have to get you out of here." He pulled his cell from his pocket and hit a couple of buttons. He spoke into the handset. "You need to get down here right now. Something's happened that will change everything."

A fresh set of nerves spiked through Autumn's stomach. Where only seconds earlier she'd been excited and disbelieving about what had just happened, she suddenly wondered if she had something to fear.

The elevator pinged open. Haverly grabbed her and pushed her behind him. Blake emerged and Haverly's grip on her loosened. Autumn's heart picked up pace for a different reason.

The big man strode in, his bright, dark eyes darting around the room. "What's happened?" he demanded.

"You're not going to believe this, but Autumn's blood contaminated her experiment samples and the human DNA shifted."

Blake looked at her, curiosity in his eyes. "Your blood made the DNA change?"

"I think so. I'd need to re-run the experiment again to make sure, but it was the only outside factor."

"We don't have time for you to replicate the experiment," said Blake. "If Haverly is right, we need to get you out of here right now."

She looked between the two men in bewilderment. "But what about General Dumas? Isn't he the one who should be told? This is what he wanted, after all."

"He's the last person who should know."

Autumn forced herself to her feet. "I demand to know what's going on here!"

Haverly went over to the computer and started to bring up files. "We can't afford to explain right now. I'll try to delete as much information as I can, but I'm pretty sure Dumas has everything backed up. He's going to figure out what happened as soon as he finds Doctor Anderson missing."

"Missing?" she said in alarm. "Why am I going missing?"

"Just go with Sergeant Wolfcollar. He'll get you to safety."

When she didn't budge, Haverly leaned over and gave Autumn a shove from behind, sending her stumbling toward Blake. He caught her, hauling her up against his massive chest. She stood there looking up into his face, her heart beating too fast and too hard, before she remembered herself. She tried to pull away, but he held her fast.

"Let go of me!"

"Not yet." He looked toward Haverly. "Stay safe and be in touch."

The older man nodded. "You too."

Autumn found herself being dragged toward the elevator by her arm, too shocked to fight back.

"The cameras are still live in the here," Blake told her. "You need to act normal. If someone suspects something is wrong, all the alarms will go."

Her heart thudded as they stood in the elevator, rising to ground level.

"We can get out through the back," he continued. "Walk quickly, but not too quickly, and stay close to me."

Blake still had hold of her arm. "Do I have any choice?" she hissed.

He spoke without looking at her, staring straight ahead. "No."

The elevator doors slid open. Ahead, the security guards sat behind the desk, the metal detector creating a barrier between them and the main entrance. *Should I yell for help?* she wondered. Yet for some reason, she kept her mouth shut.

Blake glanced to either side and then turned left, pushing through another set of doors into a long corridor. He still had hold of her arm, but she was pulled tight against his body, hiding the grip he had on her from other people. They passed a woman in a suit, her eyes giving Blake's body a cursory glance before flicking only briefly to Autumn.

As they walked at a brisk pace, she felt Blake stiffen beside her. "Dumas is coming," he said in a low voice. "He's right around the corner. We need to get out of here."

She glanced around for cameras or mirrors, something that would allow him to know Dumas' position. There was nothing. She frowned. "How do you know that? Are you psychic or something?"

He smiled grimly at the notion.

Dumas' tall, lean form appeared at the end of another corridor, his silver head bent as he spoke to two men in suits. They were deep in conversation, not yet noticing them.

"Shit!" Blake hissed under his breath. He dodged to their right, pulling her through a side door. They found themselves in a storeroom, the walls bordered by metal shelves filled with cleaning products and laundered lab coats. In the far wall, a silver hatch was embedded into the brick. Blake dropped Autumn's arm and strode over. Using the handle, he pulled the hatch open to reveal a drop beyond. The silver metal square of the interior was only visible a couple of feet down before it descended into darkness.

A laundry chute.

Autumn took one look at the black hole. "You have got to be kidding me?"

"Do you want Dumas to catch you?"

"I have no idea! Do I?"

"Absolutely not, and neither do we."

"We? Other than you and Haverly, who are *we*, exactly?"

"I don't have time to explain this to you now."

Taking her by surprise, he bent down and scooped her into his arms. She let out a shriek and battered at the thick bulk of his bicep. "Put me down, you fucking Neanderthal!"

"If you want to stay alive, you'll do exactly as I say."

"Are you threatening me?" She felt faintly ridiculous, trying to be tough when she was cradled in his arms like a baby, but she didn't know how else to act.

Any notions of tenderness vanished when he lowered her over the hole. She lunged for the edge, grabbing hold, but he gave her a shove and her grip on the edge vanished. She plunged down the smooth surface.

His voice echoed down after her. "I'm helping you."

Autumn fell from the bottom of the chute and landed on her back in a huge plastic container. Her fall was softened by a mound of dirty laboratory coats beneath her. A noise came from above and she realized if she didn't move, she was likely to be squashed. Scrambling for purchase, she wriggled out of the laundry, grabbed hold of the side of the container and hauled herself out and onto the concrete floor. She barely made it out before Blake shot from the bottom, landing on his feet in a crouch, completely in contrast to her own flailing fall.

He leapt out after her and grabbed her hand. "Let's go."

CHAPTER NINE

OUT ON THE street, Blake looked left and then right, taking a moment to consider his next move. He'd go back to his apartment and gather some things. Hopefully, no one would notice them missing right away or Haverly would be able to make some kind of excuses to throw them off the scent. That would give him enough time to consider his next move.

Blake closed his eyes briefly and concentrated on his wolf as it ran through the city's streets ahead of him. The animal's tongue lolled from his mouth, his eyes bright, adrenaline coursing through his veins. It normally existed in a state of peace, and this new threat had sent fire racing through the animal.

Go south, Blake willed his wolf. *Need transport.*

In his head, a yellow cab and the sign for North Dearborn Parkway appeared. The vehicle should be rounding the corner in approximately two minutes.

With his hand still firmly wrapped around Autumn's arm, he strode down the street.

"Hey! Where the hell are you taking me?"

She dragged her heels, trying to pull back on him. Though his strength overruled hers entirely, their awkward movements made them stand out and hindered their progress. If they were going to catch that cab, he needed to be on the corner one minute from now.

"Would you walk?" he growled.

"No!" She glared at him. "Not until you tell me what is going on and where you are taking me."

"I told you we don't have time right now. If you don't walk, I'm going to pick you up and carry you over my shoulder. Would you rather I did that?"

"You wouldn't dare."

"Want to try me?"

Damn, why did she have to be so infuriating? And why was it this woman who held the potential to change the world?

She studied his face, clearly trying to decide whether he was kidding or not. "Okay, fine," she said, realizing he wasn't joking. She started to walk, hurrying to keep up with his long strides.

The wolf flashed the image of the cab again, right down the road from them and heading their way.

"Don't move," he told her. With several long, powerful strides, he stepped into the middle of the street. A horn blared, another car swerved around him. He caught sight of the vehicle he wanted heading toward him and positioned himself in the middle of the road, right in its path.

"What the hell are you doing?" Autumn screamed at him from the sidewalk. "You're going to get yourself killed."

He ignored her.

The driver caught sight of him standing in the middle of the road and the man's eyes widened. The screech of brakes tore through his ears and someone on the sidewalk—possibly Autumn—screamed. Blake's massive hands slammed down onto the warm bonnet of the car just as it came to a standstill. Through the windshield, he focused his gaze on the man behind the wheel. The cab driver stared back at him in shock.

Blake straightened and strode around to the back. He grabbed hold of the handle and yanked open the door. A businessman sat on the backseat, his briefcase clutched in his lap, his face pale.

"Get out," Blake told him.

"What? No. Are you crazy?"

The driver twisted around in his seat, his face a mask of alarm and confusion. "This guy has a fare!"

Blake flicked open the side of his leather jacket, flashing the Beretta 9mm strapped to his hip. "It's my ride now."

The businessman's eyes widened and he nodded hastily before climbing from the car and hurrying away.

Blake straightened and motioned to where Autumn still stood, her mouth hanging open. "Come on, get in!" he yelled at her. "What the hell are you waiting for?"

She checked for traffic, shook her head as if wondering what the heck she was doing, and ran across the street to where he stood beside the open cab door.

Her blue eyes locked on his. "I think you have some serious issues," she told him.

A smile tweaked his lips. "Tell me something I haven't heard before."

She climbed in, and he got in after her. Leaning forward, he told the driver what street he wanted to be taken to.

"You're not going to shoot me, are you, mister?"

"Not as long as you don't cause me any problems."

They rode in silence. He glanced over at Autumn. She stared straight ahead, her lips pressed together, her hands clasped tight in her lap. Had this woman really succeeded where so many others had failed? If Haverly was right, from this day forward, everything could change.

They turned down his road and pulled to a stop at the sidewalk. Before getting out of the cab, Blake leaned forward and snatched the driver's ID card from where it swung from the rear view mirror. "I work for the Secret Service. If I hear one complaint about what happened here today, do not think for a moment that I won't track you down and kill you. Do you understand?"

The man's eyes were pools of shock and he nodded frantically.

"Good," said Blake, pocketing the card. "As long as we understand each other."

He sensed Autumn watching him and turned to her. Held out his hand. "I'm doing all of this to keep you safe."

She gave him a thin smile. "Sure you are."

Nevertheless, she took his hand and allowed him to help her from the vehicle. With his arm around her waist, he propelled her toward his building. From the outside, the place looked like an industrial storage unit. He opened a corrugated iron door in the side and pressed on the back of Autumn's head, forcing her to duck as they climbed inside. She shot him a glare of annoyance, but then caught sight of his apartment. Metal pipes ran across the ceiling overhead. The walls were red brick, with only a few large pictures hung—the New York Skyline in black and white, another of a full moon over the ocean, a mountain and forest landscape she didn't recognize. A couple of leather couches and a glass and chrome coffee table made up the living area. The bedroom had been built on a platform, a set of metal steps leading up to it. Light shafts had been fixed in the roof, so there were no windows, but the clever cylinders of water and chemicals allowed sunlight to filter into the space. Dust motes swirled in the streams of daylight.

From the outside, no one would know someone actually lived here.

"This is your home?" she asked, one eyebrow cocked in disbelief.

"Cozy, huh?"

She wrinkled her nose. "Err, no, not really. I can't pretend it's not impressive, though."

He crossed the floor to where a kitchenette had been built against the back wall, a black granite kitchen island separating the space from the rest of the room. "I don't know about you," he called over his shoulder, "but I could do with a drink."

"Well, I could do with you telling me what the hell is going on here."

Blake reached into a cabinet and pulled down a bottle of bourbon and two glasses. He poured a shot, downed it in one, and then refilled the glass and topped up the other one. Despite the cool demeanor he portrayed, the events of the last hour had left him shaken. He picked up both glasses and carried them over to Autumn.

Though he'd never admit it, he wished they were here in different circumstances. The sight of her standing in his apartment spoke to something deep inside him. A long time had passed since he'd had a woman here.

She folded her arms across her chest. "I don't want a drink."

He shoved the glass at her. "Just take it."

"I said I don't want a drink."

"Goddamnit, woman." He downed his own bourbon and then hers. "We don't have long. Dumas is going to realize you're missing soon enough and it will only take a quick review of the security cameras to not only see you're with me, but also that you managed to achieve what he wanted and *how* you achieved what he wanted."

"But isn't it a good thing? I mean, I have no idea how my blood managed to change the human DNA, but isn't that what everyone wanted?"

"Everyone on Dumas' side, perhaps."

She frowned. "Aren't you on Dumas' side? What sides are there?"

His face hardened. "No, I'm certainly not on Dumas' side. All he wants is to harness shifters' powers to use them for his own purposes."

Autumn pointed a finger. "There! You used that word again, *shifter*. Are you going to explain to me what a shifter is?"

He narrowed his eyes at her. "I thought you would have worked that one out for yourself. Aren't you supposed to have an IQ of 140 or something?"

She cocked her head to one side. "Well, at least I use my brain instead of relying on my muscle." She fell silent, thinking. "Okay, so a shifter is whatever the species is that my blood changes human DNA into."

"Correct."

"I still don't know what a shifter is; only what its DNA looks like."

He locked her eyes with his. "It looks like me."

She blinked in surprise. "What?"

"A shifter is a human who is able to change from their human form into that of an animal spirit guide which has attached themselves to the human spirit at some point in their lives. When the animal spirit and the human spirit merge as one to inhabit the same body, the human shifts into the form of the animal."

Autumn stared at him and then snorted in laughter. "You've got to be kidding me."

His face hardened. "Does it seem like I'm kidding?"

"You think you're one of these...shifters?"

"I don't *think* I am, I know I am. And don't act so disbelieving. You're a scientist and you've seen the proof yourself underneath a microscope. Can you doubt your own eyes?"

"I...I..." She faltered and shook her head. "This isn't science. This is science fiction."

"The other day, you told me that almost everything we now take for fact was once believed to be fiction."

"I know, but this is taking things a step too far." She pursed her lips. "I think I need that drink now."

He went back to the kitchen and poured her a shot of bourbon and himself another. His fast metabolism processed the alcohol from his system too quickly. It took a lot for him to feel the effects, probably a good thing considering the circumstances. He carried the drink back to her and she took the glass and downed it in one shot, grimacing at the taste. He watched her in amusement. He hadn't expected her to do that.

"Okay, so let me get this straight," she said, taking a deep breath. "You're telling me that not only are you one of these shifters, but that my blood has the ability to turn regular humans into animals?"

He shook his head. "Not animals. Spirit shifters."

"Spirits?"

"Yes, this is what has me worried. What we are is chosen by our spirit guides. If your blood forces that to happen, an unnatural bond will occur. There's no way of knowing how either the animal spirits or the people they bond to will react. It might send them crazy...or mean."

She laughed and ran a hand through her hair. "This whole thing sounds crazy to me. Maybe I've been asleep for the last three days and I've dreamed this whole thing."

"I can promise you this is very real. Believing it's a dream could endanger your life."

"So show me," she said, shrugging almost nonchalantly. He could tell she still didn't believe a word he was saying. "Show me how you change."

"We don't have time for this," he said in frustration. "Dumas will send people after us soon enough."

"I won't believe you unless I see it for myself."

"It will frighten you," he said, thinking of the horrific change his body went through when he shifted. Did he really want her to see that? What if she ran, or puked and passed out? He'd have to shift back and haul her out of here over his shoulder. He gave the possibility a second thought. Perhaps that would be easier than trying to get her to behave fully conscious.

He stared at her, a muscle twitching in his jaw. She stared right back, holding his gaze.

"I'm tougher than I look," she said eventually. "I've had to be."

THE POWERFUL MAN stood before her, considering her demand. She'd never felt so torn. Part of her wanted to shake her head at this whole thing and get the hell out of there. This was nuts, people didn't turn into animals! Yet she'd seen proof to a certain extent, the way the human DNA had restructured itself into something else. It was perfectly possible that the *something else* had been animal. But she had to know for sure. She had to witness it for herself.

"If you don't show me, I'll continue to doubt what you're telling me. This whole thing will be a hell of a lot easier if you just show me what you're talking about. I won't have any way of not believing you then."

"You don't want to see this," he warned. "It's the stuff of nightmares."

"I'm a big girl. It's been a long time since bad dreams kept me awake at night."

She couldn't figure out if this guy had rescued her or kidnapped her. Even though part of her wanted to run, the other part wanted to move closer to him, to feel the heat she knew would be radiating off his big, strong body, to lose herself in the intensity of his dark eyes. Whatever was true, she didn't doubt that *he* believed what he was telling her. Maybe he was crazy—out of his mind, bat-shit crazy—but she couldn't pretend what she'd been working on in the lab didn't exist. There must be a thread of truth in what he was telling her.

His shoulders sagged. "Okay, I'll do it. But don't say I didn't warn you and don't run, okay? I will catch you."

She nodded, nervous. "I won't run."

Was she about to see something that would change her view of the world forever?

Blake turned his back to her and pulled his t-shirt over his head, revealing smooth, nut-brown skin over the bulk of well-defined muscle. Every muscle in his body contracted with his movements. Intricate tribal tattoos were etched into the skin of his upper back, curving around over his shoulders. Her breath caught in her chest, her heart tripping. He tossed the shirt to the floor and lowered his hands to flick open his belt.

"What are you doing?" she asked, suddenly panicked.

He glanced over his shoulder. "I get sick of having to replace my clothes."

Her voice came out as a whisper. "Oh..."

She felt she should avert her eyes, but couldn't. She was fixated on this big, beautiful, intense man currently stripping in front of her. He unbuttoned his jeans and shrugged them from his slender hips, kicking them away to reveal a rock-hard ass and thick, lean thighs covered in a spattering of dark hair. Her mouth ran dry. Why wasn't he wearing any underwear?

Naked, apart from his tattoos, he looked back at her from over his shoulder. "You promise not to run?"

"I promise," she squeaked.

He lowered his head, the muscles in his back and shoulders straining. She heard him mutter words, but didn't catch them.

His head snapped back up and he roared in pain. Autumn jumped in fright, her heart rate stepping up a notch. She clutched her hand to her chest, as though hoping to stop the organ from beating out of her rib cage.

What am I doing? I'm standing in an industrial building with a naked man I barely know who could quite easily be out of his mind. She realized if he decided to attack her, she wouldn't stand a chance. While, at five-feet-eight, she hardly sported Mia's petite stature, this guy was at least twice her body weight.

What the hell...?

Something strange was happening to Blake's skin. Red pinpricks appeared all over his previously flawless skin, and within seconds hairs appeared. He curled back over, his body wrenched one way and then the next. A sickening cracking echoed through the room and he howled.

Stop! She cried in her horrified mind. *Stop, I believe you.* Yet nothing would come out. Her mouth had run dry, her hands gripped into tight fists. Whatever was happening was clearly hurting him and she couldn't bear to watch.

But she did.

The hairs thickened, a silvery-white coating now hiding his brown skin. His toes elongated, his fingers curling and growing. His blunt nails thickened and curled in on themselves...

Claws, she realized.

His perfect rear melded into the backs of his now fur covered-thighs, and from his coccyx something began to unfurl…

A tail.

"Oh my God," she gasped, her hand moving from her chest to her mouth. Surely she wasn't really seeing this?

Blake—or what had been Blake—was on all fours now. He's bigger, she realized, even bigger than he'd been. He swung his head to face her and she gasped and stumbled back. His face was no longer human, the last residues of humanity vanished from his features.

The biggest wolf she'd ever seen stood before her, black streaks through his silver fur. He regarded her with golden yellow eyes, a deep intelligence like nothing else she'd seen before. Her breath was caught, her heart pounding.

Her mouth opened, but she was unable to find the words.

Would he attack her?

But he made no move toward her. Instead, he lowered his massive head. Autumn forced her fear to the pit of her stomach and stepped forward, tentative, hardly able to believe what she was doing. She put out her hand and he nuzzled a wet nose into her palm. With a shaking hand, she reached out her other hand and ran her fingers through his coarse fur.

"I can't believe it's really you," she whispered. He gave a low growl. "I'm sorry I didn't believe you before."

His growled again, a low rumble from deep within his chest. But she didn't find the sound to be threatening. She felt pretty sure that if he intended to be threatening, she wouldn't have any doubt about his intentions.

He nudged her again, this time more forcefully, as though he wanted her to move away.

"Okay." She did as he wanted and stepped back, giving him his space.

The growl turned into a howl, the reverberation echoing in the huge expanse of the industrial building. She heard bones cracking again and winced at the noise, hating this was hurting him.

I did that, she thought. *He turned and put himself through this because of me.* She corrected herself. *For me.*

The fur melted from his body, revealing skin. His feet and hands shrank back, the nails reducing and flattening. His pointed nose seemed to retract, the ears folding back against his head, the tail curling between his thighs and vanishing.

Blake, fully human and naked, knelt on the floor before her, panting.

She dropped to her knees before him and reached out and placed her hand on his shoulder. Heat burned though her palm, as though he was running a fever, but she knew he wasn't. She'd touched him before and he'd been burning hot then.

He lifted his face to her, the last glow of yellow melting from the brown of his eyes.

"I believe you," she said. "I'm sorry I didn't before."

Unable to speak for the moment, he simply nodded.

She put out a hand and helped him to his feet. Strangely, she no longer felt embarrassed about his nudity, as though watching such an intense, painful, unbelievable thing somehow taken their intimacy to a new level.

Instead of being embarrassed, she reached out and placed her hands against his chest, the curve of his pectorals, just above his small, dusky-brown nipples. She ran her hands over his chest, his shoulders, down his arms, as though her body needed to confirm what her brain was telling her—that he was real.

Suddenly, he reached up and caught her wrists, stilling her hands.

"Stop!" His voice came out hoarse and he pushed her away, turning his body from her.

She realized what she'd been doing. "I'm sorry. I just needed to feel for myself that you're real."

He bent to retrieve his clothing, pulling on his jeans and t-shirt. "I'm real."

CHAPTER TEN

FROM SOMEWHERE IN the building, the shrill ring of a phone cut through the air.

Now fully dressed, Blake strode across the apartment to where he had dumped his leather jacket. He fished his cell phone from the pocket, the events of the past few minutes played through his mind. How could he not be affected by Autumn's hands running over his body like that? He'd wanted to reach out and free her hair from that prim and proper bun she wore, so the curls fell down her back. He'd wanted to lock his hand in her tresses, force her mouth to his, and kiss her hard. He'd wanted to scoop her slender body against his and press his need against her flat stomach.

That was one problem with spending so much time naked. Sometimes it was hard to hide exactly how you felt.

He hit the answer key and barked into the slender phone. "Wolfcollar."

"Blake, it's me." His mind clicked into gear. *Haverly!* "Dumas has already figured out that you've taken off with Doctor Anderson. He doesn't know the reason yet, but it won't take him long. His team is already going through the computer records in the lab."

"Shit." He glanced back over at Autumn. She watched him with wide, worried eyes.

"Did you destroy the samples yet?"

Blake thought of the slivers of glass, still inside his jacket pocket. "Not properly, though I doubt they'll be in any state considering I've been running around with them not even boxed."

"Burn them as soon as you can. We don't want Dumas getting hold of them and figuring out a way of replicating whatever is in Doctor Anderson's blood that was able to cause the shift."

"Sure." He strode into his kitchen. "I'm doing it now."

He flicked on the gas burner and then went and picked up his black leather jacket, delved in the pocket, and pulled out the two slides.

Autumn must have realized what he was about to do. "No! Stop! I need those."

"Hang on," he told Haverly, then turned to Autumn. "These things are dangerous."

"But I might never be able to replicate the experiment fully."

"Good." He dropped both slides facedown into the flames. Autumn stared, dismay written all over her face.

"Okay, it's done," he said, speaking back into the phone. "Now what?"

"You need to get the doctor somewhere safe and get rid of this phone. They're already—"

His words were cut off as the sound of shouting came in the background.

"Hang on just one minute!" Haverly yelled. Blake had the feeling he wasn't talking to him. More shouts echoed down the line and then came a crash, muffled scrapes, banging, and more yelling.

A sharp crack made Blake yank his head away from the phone. "Shit!" He put the handset back to his ear. "Haverly? You still there? Can you hear me?"

But the line was dead.

"Damn it!" Blake hung up and dropped his own phone to the floor. He lifted one heavily-booted foot and brought it down hard, again and again, smashing the item into a dozen smaller pieces.

"What did you do that for?" Autumn asked, aghast.

"Dumas' lot can track a cell. They'll be here soon."

Blake closed his eyes, focusing in on his wolf. Because of the recent shift, his guide was already near and answered him quickly. *Guard,* Blake told it. *Watch out for enemies.* He sensed his wolf's understanding, and the animal took off, patrolling the perimeter of the building at a fast trot, its head held high. Its ears were pricked for sound, nostrils flared for the scent of danger.

Blake crossed the room and climbed the set of metal stairs to the raised level that served as his bedroom. He flung open the closet and pulled out a hold-all bag containing another gun, extra ammunition, a fake ID, and a wad of cash.

"What are you doing?" Autumn called up to him.

He hoisted the bag onto his shoulder and headed back down the steps. "We can't stay here. I thought I'd kept this place a secret, but they've tracked my phone." He looked at Autumn and noted that at least she didn't have her purse with her. One less thing to worry about. "We need to get out of here."

He took her by the elbow and pulled her along.

"Where are we going?" she asked, breaking into a trot to keep up with his long strides.

"I'm not sure yet."

The image of a long black car with blacked out windows cruising by suddenly appeared in his head—his wolf warning him.

"Shit," he swore, breaking into a run. "They're already here."

She ran with him now, no longer showing the resistance she had before witnessing his shift into wolf form. Together, they ran with Blake leading to the back of his apartment. Hidden in the back wall, a smaller door was cut into the brick.

"Come on."

They ducked through and stepped out into a narrow alleyway. Industrial-sized trashcans lined the opposite wall. A couple of windows were positioned higher up, metal bars barring the way— they weren't an option for escape.

In his head appeared the image of a man in a long, dark coat, a gun held close against its folds. The man stayed close to the wall, skirting the perimeter. At the intruder's back, Blake's wolf guide growled, but there was nothing it could do in spirit form except relay information back to Blake.

"Stay here," he hissed at Autumn, pressing her against the wall. He put out a hand as though to steady her.

"Where are you going?" she hissed back.

He placed his finger against his lips. *Be quiet.*

Movement came from around the corner, the strange man moving like a cop, with his back to Blake's building. As he rounded the bend, he began to turn, but he moved too late.

Blake grabbed the man, one arm wrapped around his throat, the other knocking the gun from his hand. The weapon hit the ground with a clatter, skidding across the concrete. The man didn't even get the chance to shout out in surprise. Blake tightened his grip and a choked, strangling sound escaped from the man's throat. His feet kicked, trying to find purchase, but Blake was easily six inches taller than the attacker—not to mention immensely stronger and faster—and he didn't stand a chance. Blake knew from experience that the man's lips would be turning blue by now, his eyes bulging.

He sent a thought out to his wolf: *Are there any more?* If he was found now, he'd be shot before he even got the chance to let go of the man he held captive. In his arms, the intruder went limp.

Blake wouldn't kill the man, but he'd certainly leave him unconscious for an hour or more. He let go and the guy slumped to the floor.

His wolf sent him images, another two men around the other side of the building. But were there more on his side? He couldn't imagine them splitting up in an uneven number, one would always plan on getting the other's back.

As if Blake's suspicion had conjured him, another man—a beanie hat pulled down over his head—appeared around the corner, a gun held in both hands and pointed directly at Blake.

Blake lifted his hands in surrender.

Behind him came movement as Autumn dived for the gun the other man had dropped. The new arrival swung his weapon in her direction.

"Autumn, no!" Blake yelled, his heart lurching with fear, certain she'd be killed. But she grabbed the weapon, rolled to one side, and sat up, aiming the gun in the other man's direction. She didn't get the chance to use it. Something launched at the man's back, knocking him to the ground. His gun went off with a muffled *pop*—a silencer, Blake realized—the bullet streaking past Blake's ear.

He looked back to find Chogan sitting on top of the other man. His cousin reached down, took the man's head between both hands, and gave a hard wrench, snapping his neck.

AUTUMN GOT TO her feet, still pointing the gun which trembled in her grip. She'd never even held a weapon before, never mind fired one—she was a scientist for God's sake!—but at that moment, she hadn't doubted that she would have killed to save Blake. Her back and shoulder burned from where she'd grazed herself on the concrete while going for the gun.

"You!"

With astonishment, she realized that she recognized the guy now climbing off the dead man's body. He was the same one who had stopped her on the way home.

Blake spun to her. "You know him?"

"Yes...no...Well, he helped me the other day."

The man gave a slow grin. "You can thank me later, Cuz. For now, I think we need to get out of here."

"*We* don't need to do anything. You shouldn't even be here."

"Others are coming. We can't exactly hang out."

Autumn lowered the gun. "Others?"

Blake turned to her. "There are more men on the other side of the building. And, as much as I hate to admit it, Chogan is right."

The other man jerked his head to the left, his long black hair flowing down one shoulder. "Come on, this way."

She looked to Blake for confirmation. He nodded and held his hand out to her. She slipped her free palm into his. The heat of his skin burned through hers in the cool evening. Together, the three of them ran down the alleyway until they reached a part where the building ended and a small patch of scrubland began.

Chogan lifted up a part of a chain-link fence which separated them from freedom. "Quick, under here."

He climbed through first and then Blake pushed Autumn after. She clambered beneath on her hands and knees, her hair catching in the metal wire. Pain spiked through her scalp as she tore free, her hair unraveling from the knot she'd so carefully styled first thing that morning, leaving her curls hanging around her face. She lifted her head to find Chogan standing above her. The strange man reached down to help her up. She hesitated a moment, wondering if she could trust this new arrival, but took the offered hand and allowed him to pull her to her feet.

Blake rolled beneath, a smooth movement for such a big man, and he pulled the fence back down, hiding the hole.

"They're coming," he hissed.

They stepped back into the dark shadows of the alcove of the adjacent building just as two more men, both carrying weapons, ran past on the other side of the fence. The small group waited for a moment for them to pass by, and then Chogan slid out of the shadows and took off across the patch of scrubland.

Autumn and Blake exchanged a glance and followed.

The area led out onto another street. They slowed to a fast walk so as not to stand out.

"We don't need you here, Chogan," said Blake, keeping his voice low. "This doesn't concern you."

"Could have fooled me. You'd probably be shot in the head right now if I hadn't come along. Why are they after you, anyway?"

"It's none of your business."

"No? Well, why do I have the feeling this has something to do with the missing shifters you were supposed to be checking up on?"

Autumn looked between the two men like she was at a tennis match. "Missing shifters? You mean, like you are?" she asked Blake.

Chogan interrupted. "Like we both are."

Her eyes widened. "You too?"

"Yes." He studied her. She shifted uncomfortably under the intensity of his gaze, so like Blake's, but with a sharper edge. "And where exactly do you come into all of this?"

Blake growled. "She doesn't."

"No? Don't lie to me, Cuz. I can smell your lies coming off you like bad cologne."

Blake's hand pressed against the small of her back, the contact making her draw in a breath of surprise. "I don't have time to explain all of this. Dumas' men are going to discover the apartment empty, not to mention an unconscious man and a dead body, and figure out that we've been there and can't be far. We need to concentrate on getting to safety and talk then."

Chogan seemed to weigh up his options. "Fine. I've got a hotel room. We can hole up there for the time being, and then you can tell me why these people want you and Blondie dead."

Autumn's head snapped around at the name. "Actually, it's Doctor Anderson to you."

He smirked and she got a glimpse of impossibly white teeth. "Is it now? Beauty *and* brains. My favorite combination."

CHAPTER ELEVEN

THANKS TO THE wonder of Google, it hadn't taken Mia long to pull up the position of the Wests' apartment. Only one park lay in close proximity to their home, so this was where she intended to start her search for their missing son.

She pulled her old, red Honda Civic into the parking lot opposite the old pavilion in Thatcher Woods then climbed out and headed off down one of the paths more often used by joggers or dog-walkers. The hour was getting late now, so she didn't pass many other people. She'd wanted to try to capture what Toby might have been feeling or doing, while still being able to see. Her feet sank into the muddy ground of the floodplain, the Des Plaines River rushing peacefully by. On either side of her, oak trees rose gracefully into the sky, the wind rustling their branches as though they were taking part in a whispered conversation she wasn't privy too. Mia wasn't even sure what she was looking for— some kind of clue that might lead to the explanation of why Toby left his room in the middle of the night and where he was now.

Due to the river running through the area, Thatcher Woods often suffered from flooding, which would explain the presence of the muddy footprints and Toby's dirty feet. Of course, it still didn't explain how he was getting in and out of his room in the middle of the night, but she hoped that would come to light.

She spotted the green shirt and tan sunhat of one of the volunteers who helped maintain the park.

"Excuse me?"

The older man turned to her with a scowl until he caught sight of the young, pretty woman, and then his face brightened. He cleared his throat and wiped his palms on the front of his shirt. "Oh, hello, Miss. Can I help you?"

Mia pulled a photograph of Toby West from her purse. "I wondered if you might have seen this boy. He's been missing for nine days now, and he liked to come to the woods."

He peered in at the photograph. "Missing, you say?"

She nodded.

"No, I'm sorry, can't say I have."

"It's possible he came here at night time."

His lips pursed, his fat forehead furrowing in disapproval. "Night time?"

She knew what he was thinking. The group of volunteers who maintained the park had recently removed a dilapidated concrete shelter from the woods to try to prevent groups of delinquents from gathering and drinking and taking part in not-so-welcome activities.

"Oh, no, not like that," she said hurriedly. "He just liked to walk."

"Hmm, well, I'm sorry, but he doesn't look familiar to me."

"Are you working with others today? Might they be willing to take a look?"

"Sure, though I think a few of them have probably called it a day. The rest will be all over the park. Might take you a while to get around them."

The park covered more than two hundred acres. Traipsing around trying to find a few persons would be like searching for individual pebbles on a beach. "Is there any way you can contact them for me? Perhaps ask them to meet me when they're done?"

"I suppose that would be okay." He pulled a cell from his pocket and placed a number of calls.

"Thanks," she said, offering him a smile.

He shrugged. "No problem. Though they might be awhile."

She thanked him again and kept herself busy by continuing her walkabout until the other volunteers showed up. She noticed surveillance cameras around the parking lot and restrooms, and wondered who she'd need to contact to gain access to the footage. There was a chance they might have picked up something.

Gradually, a couple of other volunteers showed up and Mia ran through the same questions again. The result was the same. None had seen Toby or recognized his photograph. She sighed. It really did seem like he'd vanished into thin air.

The last of the light began to vanish from the sky, the moon appearing as a ghostly circle in the indigo sky.

Time to call it a day.

Mia headed back to her car. Other than a couple of vehicles belonging, she assumed, to the volunteers, the parking lot was empty. She reaching into her purse and fished out her keys. As she reached her car, and went to select the correct key to open the door, she fumbled the key fob and dropped them on the asphalt. She bent to pick them up again.

As she straightened, rough hands grabbed her by the shoulders and spun her around, pinning her against the side of her car. She drew in a breath to scream, but a hand blocked her mouth. She found herself staring into the gray eyes of her attacker. Though she couldn't see any other part of the man's features, she noted distinctive gold flecks in the iris of his right eye. A black balaclava, like the type she'd expect to see in an old hold-up movie, covered the rest of his face.

Immediately, her worst fear sprang to mind. *Oh, God. I'm going to be raped.* But then the man reached for her purse and she wondered if he planned on mugging her first.

Her eyes flicked over his shoulder, desperately hoping someone else was around—if not one of the volunteer rangers, then a dog walker or jogger—but the place seemed to be deserted.

To her confusion, he reached into her purse and pulled out the photograph of Toby West. He crumpled the picture in front of her face. "Stop asking about the boy," he spat. "I'm warning you."

The man let her go and spun on his heels, taking off at a jog across the car lot and disappearing between the trees.

He left her gasping with shock, the world blurring as tears filled her eyes. Sudden panic filled her as she wondered if he'd come back and finish the job, and she hit the button on her key fob to open the car. She fumbled with the handle a couple of times before dragged the door open, climbing inside, and slamming the door behind her. She locked the doors, her hands shaking.

What the hell? Why on earth would someone warn her off asking about Toby? The only explanation was that the man had something to do with the boy going missing, but how would he know who she was or where she'd be? Also, that was pretty unusual behavior for someone who might be involved in the disappearance. Normally, she'd expect a perp to stay well out of the way, not confront someone in the daytime, and in a public place at that. The whole thing was off.

She'd need to report the incident to the police, preferably the detective dealing with the case. If the person responsible for Toby going missing was still in the city, then there was a good chance Toby was as well.

She took a deep breath and settled her hands on the wheel. Right now, she only wanted to be home. Safe. With people around her she trusted.

CHAPTER TWELVE

CHOGAN'S HOTEL ROOM was clean and tidy, but modest. A double bed was neatly made, a small bottle of water positioned next to a glass on the bedside table. On the desk, opposite the bed, was a small flat screen television. None of his belongings littered any of the surfaces, no change of clothing or toiletries on the desk.

"How did you get to the city?" Blake asked him, thinking he already knew the answer.

"I ran," he replied, confirming Blake's suspicions. Being in wolf form made it difficult to carry luggage.

Blake nodded his understanding. As wolves, they were able to move quickly and almost silently through the areas unpatrolled by police or security cameras. Taking wolf form wasn't a bad idea. They could stay off the radar that way. Dumas' men were less likely to find them than if they took a car and rode the highway.

Autumn's complexion was pale and she sank down to sit on the edge of the bed.

"Are you all right?" Blake asked her, frowning.

She nodded. "This is all just a lot to take in."

He reached out and picked up the bottle of water, twisted off the cap, and handed it to her. "Here, drink this."

She accepted the water with a grateful smile.

"We should be safe here for the time being," said Chogan. "So are you going to tell me what's going on?"

Blake hesitated. He'd not seen Chogan for several years, and they'd not parted company on good terms. He didn't trust the other shifter, even though they were blood related. But right now, he didn't have the luxury of being picky; he wasn't exactly swimming in allies. His thoughts turned to Haverly. He hoped the other man was all right.

The problem was the last time he had spoken to Chogan, his cousin hadn't exactly shared his—and most other shifters'—views about keeping their kind a secret. In Chogan's mind, the world would be a better place if all humans were aware of the existence of their kind. He believed them to be stronger and more powerful than the rest of humanity. He didn't seem to comprehend the fact that they would be forced to live like freaks.

Blake decided half the truth would have to do. There was no need for his cousin to learn about the reason behind Dumas' interest in Autumn. The idea made him shudder. God only knows what Chogan would do with such information.

"The department I work for is holding three shifters captive," he said, running a hand over the top of his head. Unable to contain his frustration, he began to pace the small floor space of the hotel room. Chogan stood by the window, his arms folded, his expression hard.

Autumn straightened, her eyes wide. "What?"

He'd forgotten this would be news to her as well. "I think one of them is the woman you were talking about, Chogan, the one from the reservation. She shifted into a panther. Does that sound right?" He looked to him for confirmation. From the way the other man stood, with his fists clenched, jaw tight as he glared at him, Blake assumed it did.

"I'll kill the bastards," his cousin spat.

Autumn leaned forward, her elbows rested on her knees, hands knotted together. "Where are they held captive?"

"Containment Area Three. The bottom level beneath the building."

"The one only accessible by the fingerprint pad?"

He nodded. "Right. Other than via the elevator, no one can get down there, so freeing them won't be easy. The only possibility might be via tunnels which run beneath the building. They're designed as a way to get Dumas and anyone else he considers important enough out, should the building come under some kind of attack. I'm not sure how we'd do it alone, but a distraction on the upper level might mean one of us could get to the shifters from below."

"Okay," Chogan nodded slowly, "I think we can work with that. But how did they get the woman from the reservation to shift? She's not a birth shifter, she shouldn't be able to shift at will."

Blake hung his head and chewed at his lower lip. "Dumas and his men are torturing them to get them to shift. Electric shocks. They've got a boy as well—no more than fourteen, maybe fifteen years old. The woman shifted in order to stop the boy being tortured. They had her chained with cuffs on her wrists and legs and she broke every limb while she shifted."

Chogan turned away, shaking his head. "Jesus ..."

Autumn stared at him in horror. "They're torturing people? Right beneath where I was working? How the hell could you let them?"

His head snapped around at her. "What was I supposed to do? I needed to find out what Dumas had planned. I needed to keep an eye on what you were doing." He glared at her, hoping she'd understand he didn't want her to share that particular part of the story with their new companion.

She seemed to understand and backed down.

Chogan lifted his chin in her direction. "So what's she got to do with this whole thing?"

"She's nothing. She just got caught up in the wrong place at the wrong time."

He looked between them, as if trying to decide if this was the truth.

"Well, what do we do now?" asked Autumn.

"Sit pretty until we figure out what to do," said Blake. "Rest up."

Chogan growled. "I'm not going to sit around and do nothing."

"We can't do anything until the heat dies down," Blake snapped. "So just cool it."

Hoping for distraction, he crossed the room and flicked on the television. A news article came on, nothing interesting. Then another reporter interrupted and a news reel ran across the bottom of the screen …

"Breaking news. Local police in Chicago are warning citizens to be on their guard for this man…" A picture of Blake, sullen and threatening, flashed up on screen. *"He is thought to be armed and dangerous after kidnapping renowned scientist, Doctor Autumn Anderson."* Now it was Autumn's turn to have her face flashed on screen—a photograph of her, probably taken for a work ID at some time, wearing her suit and glasses, looking older than she did now. The reporter continued, *"Sergeant Blake Wolfcollar kidnapped Doctor Anderson from the government building where she was working this afternoon, attacking one man and killing another. If you have any information about his whereabouts, please contact the number on screen below."* The reporter lowered his notes and peered intently into the camera. *"Please, whatever you do, do not be tempted to approach this man yourself. He is armed and considered extremely dangerous."*

Blake stared around. "You have got to be fucking kidding me."

Chogan looked to Autumn with fresh suspicion in his eyes. "So what are they so caught up about you for Blondie. A scientist, huh? What kind of scientist?"

Blake glared at her, but this time she didn't get the hint. "I'm a molecular geneticist."

"So, basically someone who works on DNA?" His eyes narrowed. "What are you not telling me, Cuz?"

"Nothing." Blake scowled.

Chogan gave a half-smile. "Now why do I not believe that?"

AUTUMN COULD BARELY believe she'd just seen herself on television. And for them to say Blake had killed someone… Well, she knew the report was untrue. Chogan had been the one who killed a man.

"I need to let my dad know I'm safe," she said. "And Mia, my roommate. They'll be so worried if they see the news." With a deep-rooted sadness, she realized she didn't have many other people in her life who would be worried about her. She'd spent so much time focused on her work, she'd not spent any on cultivating new friendships, or relationships even. In fact, it had been a long time since she'd been in a hotel room with any man, never mind two.

"You can't contact anyone," said Blake. "Dumas will probably have people stationed close to your family and home. It'll be the first place he'll think you'll go."

Chogan butted in. "And why is the government so interested in her again?"

Blake ignored him. "We'll be safe here for the time being. We need to consider our next move."

"Our next move is going and getting those shifters out," said his cousin.

Blake shook his head. "It's not so simple."

"Sounds simple to me."

"I can't risk taking Autumn back there."

"Why not?"

"She might get hurt."

Chogan locked a hand in his long hair and gave an exasperated sigh. "Fine, we'll leave her here. I still don't understand why you've dragged her along anyway."

Blake scowled. "She was involved. I couldn't just abandon her."

"No, but you can leave her now."

"That's a government facility, Chogan. Do you really think they're going to let you waltz in and set three shifters free after what Dumas has done to them? There's security on every door, cameras in every corner."

"I thought you were supposed to be part of that security?"

"I am. And I know the place better than anyone. You're not getting in there right now. Anyway, I can't leave Autumn on her own."

Chogan appraised her, his eyes roving up and down her body. She didn't think much of the way the two men were having a discussion around her instead of with her. She thinned her lips and did her best to hold herself back from punching him in the head.

He smirked. "Why not? She looks like a big girl. I'm sure she can take care of herself."

Autumn straightened, her eyebrows cocked. "I am here, you

know!" she snapped. She didn't know who to be madder at, but she turned to Blake. "He's right. I can."

"I don't care. I'm not leaving you here alone. You're too… important…" He stumbled over his words.

She noted the color in his cheeks and the way he glanced away from her, and felt sure he'd been about to say something else.

"Well, I'm not hanging around here," said Chogan, heading for the door. "You two hide away here, but I'm going to find out what the hell is going on."

CHAPTER THIRTEEN

CHOGAN STEPPED FROM the hotel and paused to assess his surroundings. The government building was located on the other side of the city, but he didn't intend to catch a cab. One of his strengths was being able to run—even in human form—and he enjoyed doing so. Besides, being on foot would give him time to think. Something wasn't quite right with his cousin's story about the blonde scientist, though he couldn't figure out what part was off. The woman wasn't one of them, he knew that much, but at the same time, there seemed to be something else about her. She gave off a kind of radiance he found himself drawn to, and, by the look of things, Blake reacted to her in the same way.

It wouldn't be the first time the two of them had been interested in the same woman, and the situation hadn't worked out well the last time. In fact, things couldn't have ended any worse. The memory still managed to invoke a fresh stab of pain. The events of almost ten years ago had been the final straw for Blake, the thing that had finally caused him to turn his back on their family and leave for good. He'd initially joined the army, which led him to his role now.

He was aware that Blake held him to blame about what happened all those years ago, and in a way he couldn't blame him. But, whatever Blake believed, Chogan couldn't help but feel like his cousin should never have turned his back on his own.

As he ran through the streets, people gave him strange glances. Not often did they see a six-foot-tall Native American with long hair running through the city.

Having his cousin's face plastered all over the news didn't help matters. People might catch a glimpse of him and perhaps confuse him with Blake. Even though they were distinctly different in body size and temperament, people who'd only ever caught Blake's face on television might get them confused.

Chogan focused into himself and connected with his wolf; a big, ferocious animal, always quick to react, ready to shift whenever needed. His wolf liked him to be in wolf form, wanted to be at one with the rest of the world. Chogan sensed being in spirit form frustrated the animal, and sometimes he had to mentally hold his wolf off from forcing him to shift.

Being on the reservation, though surrounded by forest and animals to hunt, the wolf grew restless with the lack of new stimulation. Even though they were surrounded by concrete now, he got the sense his spirit guide was enjoying the challenge of this new hunt.

The wolf ran ahead.

Only a block from the government building, Chogan drew to a stop. His wolf placed several images in his head—a group of people standing outside the building, surrounding the steps leading up to the unmarked blacked-out glass doors. On top of the steps stood a man with silvery-white hair who wore an expensive suit and a grim expression. Several flashes of bright light made Chogan blink and raise his hand to shield his eyes, as though the action would make a difference. The bright lights he saw were inside his head.

Reporters. He guessed they were present for the apparent kidnapping of the scientist his cousin was now holed up with in his hotel room.

Damn. With all those people hanging around, he wouldn't be able to get close to the building. He'd need to send his wolf inside, though the farther his wolf travelled from him, the weaker their connection became.

Still, he decided, getting some idea of the layout of the building would be better than having none at all.

Go, he instructed his guide. *Into the building and down to the lowest level.*

His wolf growled and leapt forward, passing, unnoticed by the crowd of people, through the door.

Chogan received information in a reel of images in his head. More security stood on the inside. An elevator, a set of doors, a corridor, more people in suits hurrying as though the weight of the world was on their shoulders.

Go down.

His wolf was still tied to the real world, it couldn't fly or dive beneath water for long periods of time. Though able to pass through walls and doors as if they didn't exist, it couldn't jump down an elevator shaft of several stories. There had to be another way to the bottom level.

His wolf slowed its pace. It walked with its nose close to the floor, searching for another way down, but, as Blake had said, the only way seemed to be via the elevator.

The wolf lifted its head and whined as someone approached. Long, authoritative strides, suit jacket flapping with the man's motion. The wolf sent Chogan the image of the same man who'd been stood on the steps. Was this the one Blake had mentioned about being linked to the capture and torture of the other shifters? Dumas?

The man entered the elevator and pressed his finger to a screen on the right of the keypad.

Go! Chogan willed.

He sensed the wolf's reluctance, but it followed, and the elevator headed down. The doors opened and the man walked out, unaware of the wolf hot on his heels.

They passed into a room filled with a panel of computers. A couple of people at the panel monitoring something beyond turned to nod at Dumas as he walked in. The wolf rose on its haunches, front paws placed on the panel to see over the top. A glass screen divided the computers and men from what lay beyond. Three people were held captive. His wolf growled and, in unison, all of the shifters lifted their heads.

Chogan wished he could hear what was being said. The men were obviously talking to one another, but due to the distance between him and his wolf, he was unable to pick up their words.

The state of the captives made him furious. Each of them sported blackened eyes and abrasions, and the woman had each of her arms and legs bound in thick support bandages. They were no longer tied, but instead each huddled in a corner of their own personal cell. A metal chair stood in the center of each of the cells. The source of the electroshock treatment, he assumed.

How had his cousin been a part of this? How could he stand by and do nothing while these people were being hurt?

Anger boiled up inside him. Blake had always made out like he was the injured party, the one who always played the good guy to his bad, but now here were people who he'd allowed to be harmed.

Using all his mental strength to keep the bond with his wolf strong, even at hundreds of feet through the earth, he urged his wolf forward, through the panels of glass and into the individual glass cells with the captive shifters. Though his wolf could do nothing physical, he placed a wet nose into each captive's hands in turn, nuzzling with hot wolf-breath, trying to offer just a little comfort.

I'll get you out, he promised them silently. *However many of these sons of bitches I need to kill to do it.*

BLAKE PACED AROUND the hotel room, his fists clenched at his sides.

"Will you sit down?" said Autumn. "You're making me anxious."

"You should be anxious. Dumas won't have any qualms about picking you up off the street, faking your death—probably blaming it on me at the same time in order to get me out of the picture—and then holding you captive for the rest of your life. Is that really what you want?"

She looked at him in alarm. "No! Of course not, but I still don't understand why he'd want me."

"I thought I'd explained this to you already? I thought you understood."

She held her hands out either side of her body and arched her eyebrows. "Obviously not."

He sighed and sat down on the edge of the bed, only a foot of air separating their bodies.

"There are things you need to know about shifters, Autumn. My kind are extremely secretive, and we go out of our way not to interact with each other. By not gathering as a group, we remain unnoticed."

"Until now," she said.

He nodded. "Until now."

"So how does it work if you all stay apart from each other? How are more spirit shifters born?"

"You misunderstand. Our gift—or curse—isn't something that can be passed down from generation to generation. Instead, our spirits choose us."

She frowned. "They choose you? How?"

"When a new soul is born in the world, the spirit will recognize the one it is supposed to be with. Sometimes, like in my case, this happens at birth. My spirit guide was already waiting for me and we became joined as soon as I was born. Of course, the strengths, like my ability to shift into the form of my spirit guide—in my case, a wolf—didn't come until we grew stronger together and learned how to work together. Others aren't chosen until later in life, and those shifters are much weaker, but they are still stronger and faster and have abilities far greater than a regular human."

Autumn could barely believe she was going to ask this, especially with her own dubious religious views, but she had to know. "Does having a guide mean you're somehow connected to God?"

He gave a short, humorless laugh. "Not at all. There's no higher power working here other than spirituality. Not organized religion, just the power of nature."

"But if the spirits choose the person they bind to, then surely that person must be some kind of spiritual soul. They must have goodness at their hearts."

"Not always. Not all spirits are good, just as not all people are good. Evil exists in all planes of our world."

"I don't understand. Those who are chosen at birth … how would a spirit know when a newborn is going to turn out to be a bad adult?"

"A soul is a soul and will always be who they are, regardless of outside forces. Why do you think people who are brought up in exactly the same situation can grow up acting in two completely different ways? Take two children who grow up in abusive families. One child might grow up to be abusive himself, while the other grows up working for organizations to try to prevent such a thing happening to others. If someone has evil at their core, they'll be that person, no matter what."

She arched her eyebrows. "Well, that's an ongoing debate—nurture versus nature. Most people put it down to genetics, not the person's soul."

A small smile played on his lips. "I wouldn't expect you to say anything else. For the most part, you'd be right, but not always."

"So, where do I come into this?"

"When our spirit guides bind to us, something changes about our molecular make-up. As a human, our genetics are human, but when we start to shift, our genes change too."

"Your genetic sequences rearrange," Autumn said, her understanding slotting into place. "Dumas is trying to replicate a shifter's genes from human DNA."

Blake nodded. "All shifters—even in human form—have better senses than any human alive. Plus, we're faster, stronger, and heal more quickly. But that's not all. Those who are well-synched with their spirit guides can view the world through their eyes, even when in human form. I can send my wolf ahead of me for several miles, and though he's invisible to everyone else, I'm able to see what he's seeing."

She looked at him in wonder. "That's amazing. So can you see something else right now?"

"Let's not get distracted by what I can and can't do. We need to worry about what Dumas wants with spirit shifters, and, because of what you did, what he now wants with you."

"Dumas wants to be able to create shifters from regular humans, but why?"

"I thought you were smart, Autumn."

She briefly closed her eyes, putting the final pieces of the puzzle together. "He wants spirit shifter strengths."

"Yes, though not for himself. Imagine an army who can not only move faster and are stronger than their enemies, and whose injuries heal within hours, but who can also send eyes and ears into enemy territory without anyone ever knowing they're there."

"An army of spirit shifters?"

He nodded. "No one has ever been able to achieve what you have, Autumn. Many have tried—not that the other scientists survived their failures."

Her eyes widened in alarm. "What do you mean?"

"Accidents, if you can call them that. When previous scientists failed to get any further in their research, or perhaps they'd learned too much, they tended to meet with unfortunate accidents."

"Like who?" she demanded. "Who were these scientists?"

"Before you was an older professor called Cordell."

"William Cordell?"

He nodded.

"William Cordell suffered a heart attack. He died in his sleep. The news was well-circulated in the scientific community."

"Certain drugs have the ability to induce a heart attack and make it appear natural."

"Who else?"

"Before him was Doctor Laurence Holt."

Autumn thought for a moment, trying to place a face with the name. Then she remembered who Blake was talking about. She'd met with him briefly at a conference in New York.

"I wasn't aware he'd died."

Blake nodded. "Car accident. Not very original, but they happen all the time."

She paused before asking the question burning at her heart. She didn't want to insult him, but considering his position, she needed to know. "Were you involved in their deaths?"

He held her gaze. "No, Autumn, I wasn't. Though I wonder if I should have done more to try to save them."

"Like you're doing with me now?"

"You're different."

"Am I?"

Tension buzzed between them. He spoke softly. "You know you are."

"The ability to change the DNA might not be specific to my blood. Blood in general might cause the DNA to shift?"

Blake shook his head. "No, I'm sure those tests would already have been done. If we still had access to the files and could get back into the lab, we might be able to find out. I'm certain Dumas won't destroy the research."

Autumn considered this. "Okay, say the test with blood has already been done, how can we be sure some other outside influence, some other contaminant, didn't affect the results?"

He studied her face and she shifted uncomfortably under his intense, dark stare. "There's something special about you, Autumn. I noticed from the first moment I saw you. Don't tell me you've gone through life feeling like everyone else?"

Her cheeks colored. Of course she hadn't. Her mom had died when she was young, she had a reclusive scientist, who had no idea how to handle teenage girls, for a father, and she'd grown up smarter than any of the kids in her class. No one liked the class geek. Even being moved up a year hadn't helped. Then, she even made the other geeks look bad. As for boys...well … She shuddered at the memory. Her following the boys she liked around like some lost puppy. Them, always older than her, looking down at her—at least in the metaphorical sense, she'd been tall and gangly even back then—and laughing.

She broke the moment, not answering the question. "Surely there is something else we can do? Go to the press or something?"

"And tell them what? You'd look like a crazy person. Plus, the government owns everyone. No one would dare expose them for having people murdered, but what they would do is expose the existence of my kind. If the world knew about us, we'd be turned into freaks or monsters. Vigilante groups would try to hunt us down. We'd be locked up in far more science labs than what Dumas and his team have done."

She allowed the implication of what he'd said to sink in. Something else occurred to her.

"So is your wolf spirit here now? Listening to us?" She couldn't help but find the idea slightly freaky, as though she no longer had her privacy.

He shook his head. "My spirit guide doesn't watch me, but the world around me. That way, it can guide me when needed, show me danger, or warn me of something."

"What does it feel like? Does your spirit guide speak in your head? Can wolves even speak?"

Blake laughed. "No, of course not. No more than any other wolf can speak. But my wolf shows me things, put images or smells in my head."

"All the time? Any time he wants?"

Again he shook his head. His gaze drifted away from her for a moment as he considered what he was about to say. "Have you ever been asleep and dreaming, only for someone to talk to you or the phone ring, and the sound somehow infiltrates your dream? You know it's happening and your body fights to either wake up or ignore the noise. Well, that's what it's like for me all of the time. In the back of my mind, I can feel my wolf, what it's seeing or feeling, and I can either choose to wake up and fully connect, or else I can choose to sleep and not open my mind."

She smiled. "It's interesting that you compare blocking your mind off to your guide as like being asleep."

He shrugged. "I'm never more awake than when I connect completely, especially when we go that step further and become one."

"When you become a wolf?" Her voice was hushed with awe.

"When the wolf and I become one."

"That's amazing, you know."

His gaze smoldered. "You're amazing."

She glanced away, the heat in her face deepening in intensity. "But how is it possible that I'm able to do what you say, if I even accept that what you're saying is right? I mean, I can kind of understand you being able to do what you do—even though I've had to seriously rethink some of my beliefs—because of who you are, you know, your...culture."

He cocked an eyebrow. "You mean because I'm Native American."

She bit her lower lip, worrying at a piece of dried skin. "Well...yes. Isn't the existence of spirit guides something you've been brought up with, something your culture has believed for centuries?"

"Autumn, just because one culture has embraced a part of life, doesn't mean it doesn't exist in other cultures as well. We just learned to accept and embrace it as a part of our lives. It was never hidden away, but the rest of the world simply assumed something like that couldn't be true. Of course, those able to shift into the form of their guides were never paraded around. They would have been taken away and treated like freaks—"

"Like how Dumas is doing now," she interrupted.

Blake's features darkened to a scowl. "Exactly. Which is why I have to figure out a way to save those people."

"You will," she said, and then corrected herself. "*We* will."

He shook his head. "You're not going anywhere near that place. God knows what will happen if Dumas gets hold of you. He can make you vanish from the face of the earth."

Her eyes widened. "He can't do that! I have family who will ask questions, friends and colleagues who will wonder where I am. They'll go to the police."

"It won't make a difference, Autumn. If he wants to bleed you dry in order to change as many people as possible, that's exactly what he will do. He'll tell other people in authority you're needed for the security of this country, and they won't say a thing. Everyone lives in fear now, and if he says you're needed to make our country safer from the threat of terrorism, no one will question him."

The pressure in Autumn's head increased, making it feel as though her heart was thumping in her temples. "But that's insane."

Suddenly, the walls of the small hotel room seemed to be closing in around her, her chest tightening, heart pounding. Breath whistled in and out of her lungs and she struggled to catch it. The only driving force inside her was a desperate knowledge that she needed to get out, and needed to get out now.

She jumped to her feet and rushed for the door, the floor tilting beneath her feet like a ship in a storm. *People she knew were dead. Men could turn into animals. Someone wanted to capture her and do God-knows-what.*

She managed to get to the door and reached for the handle, but her spinning mind couldn't seem to focus on where her fingers needed to be to get the door open. She was only barely aware of movement behind her, of Blake calling her name, concern thickening his voice.

"Autumn! Autumn, wait!"

Then his hands were on her shoulders, turning her to him. She locked her gaze on his deep dark eyes, her mind taking focus on the only solid thing in the room. Before she could process what was happening, his mouth was on hers, crushing the breath from her lungs for a different reason this time. His arms wrapped around her back, holding her against the solid heat of his body. How he held her! Never had she been caught in the grip of such a powerful man before, as if every inch of his body was coiled muscle, and she found herself being grounded by his strength. The heat of his mouth burned against hers. Her fingers locked around his neck, reaching into the soft hair at his nape. Seemingly of their own accord, her hands traced his skin, running down the thick cords of his throat and across his massive shoulders. All panic fled her mind as he kissed her deeper, his tongue entwining with her own. She pressed herself into the hard planes of his body, wanting to lift herself up and wrap her thighs around his narrow hips and forget everything else that was happening.

They broke apart, gasping, staring at each other with a new kind of wonder. Blake reached out, his fingers cupping her cheek. His skin burned. But he shook his head and lowered his eyes.

"I'm sorry, Autumn. I shouldn't have done that."

"What? Why not?"

"This is all too complicated as it is." He took her hand and led her back to the bed. Her heart stuttered at their proximity to clean sheets and a soft mattress, but he took a seat on the very edge, leaning forward with his elbows pressed into his thighs, his fingers pressed into his temples.

"I'm scared, Blake," she said, finally admitting to herself that it was the truth.

"You should be. Dumas is a dangerous man."

"So he can take me and no one will ever know what happened?"

He lifted his head and locked his dark eyes on her. A shiver ran through her body. "I'll know what happened. And I won't rest until you're safe."

CHAPTER FOURTEEN

THE DOOR OF the hotel room burst open and Autumn quelled a shriek of surprise. Chogan's form filled the gap. His eyes were hooded with anger, his forehead drawn down in a frown. The other man took three long strides across the room and caught his cousin by the material of his shirt, hoisting the bigger man to his feet and propelling him backward. The two men hit the hotel room wall, a picture knocking from a hook and falling to the floor with a crash, and the scream finally escaped Autumn's throat.

"What the hell are you involved with?" Chogan demanded.

Blake pushed back, the initial advantage of surprise gone. Chogan stumbled briefly, but quickly regained himself, leaping to his feet and squaring on Blake like two men in a wrestling ring.

"I don't know what you're talking about."

"Bullshit! I saw those poor shifters, what they'd done to them. How could you be involved with someone who is doing that to your own kind? What the hell do those people want from them?"

"They're just trying to find out what we are."

Chogan snarled. "I don't believe you. There's more to it."

Terrified they'd hurt each other, Autumn jumped to her feet. She positioned herself between the two men, hands held out, placed against their chests to separate them. The same heat which radiated from Blake also came from his cousin's skin.

She turned to Blake. "If he's like you, why don't you tell him the whole story?"

"Damn it, Autumn!" Blake glared at her.

Chogan leapt on their exchange. "So I'm right. There is more to this."

Blake paused and then grabbed Autumn's hand and dragged her outside into the corridor. A small Hispanic woman wheeling a trolley of clean sheets and mini toiletries passed them by. She gave them a sideways glance, but nothing more.

Autumn snatched her hand from his and put her hands on her hips. "So are you going to explain to me what your beef is with your cousin? It seems to me like he only wants to help, and we're not exactly overwhelmed by people wanting to help us right now."

"You have no idea what he's like."

"No, I don't. So why don't you tell me?"

Blake turned from her slightly and ran a hand across his buzz cut hair. He shook his head as though fighting an inner battle, then opened his mouth to speak. "Chogan doesn't consider himself—or any of the shifters—on an equal level with humans. He thinks our abilities make us a higher species. He thinks humans should know about us, should bow down and worship us. That's part of the reason he's so furious about the other shifters being held captive. In his head, it's like the masters being held and tortured by the slaves."

"Wow."

He looked grim. "Yeah, wow. I don't know how he's going to react to the news that you might be able to change humans into shifters. It could go one of two ways—he sees you as the messiah and wants to try to change as many people into shifters as possible, or he'll view you as the anti-Christ who is about to reduce our kind to nothing."

"Okay, neither of those are good reactions," she said, slowly. "But other than hoping he'll help us, what other options do we have?"

"We go it alone."

"For how long? We barely know each other. I can't just go on the run with some strange man for God-knows-how-long. I have a job! I have a life."

Blake glanced away, as if suddenly uncomfortable. "I'm sorry, but your life just changed."

She stared at him, hardly able to believe what he was saying. Had her old life really ended? It was all too much to handle.

"I still don't think we can do this alone, whatever *this* is." She remembered Chogan's kindness upon finding her crying in the street after her latest confrontation with her father. "I want Chogan to know what's going on. The full story."

"You don't know what he's like," Blake warned again.

"You said you'd not seen each other for a long time. Maybe he's changed?"

Blake gave a sigh, his huge shoulders sagging, and Autumn knew she'd won this argument at least.

"Anyway," she said, looking around the cramped corridor. "If he's like you, can't he just use his spirit guide to listen in on this conversation?"

He shook his head. "It's an unspoken law between shifters that we don't watch each other. Imagine the total lack of privacy you'd go through your whole life otherwise. Besides, my wolf would know if Chogan's was here."

"Okay, but I still think we need to tell him."

"Fine. But if this all goes horribly wrong, don't say I didn't warn you."

They went back into the room.

Chogan stood, his hands shoved into the pockets of his jeans. He looked up at them as they walked in. "You two finished your little mothers' meeting?"

"Yeah," said Blake. He motioned with his head toward the bed. "And if you want to hear what we have to say, I suggest you sit down and shut the hell up."

Chogan gave them a tight smile. "I guess I don't have much choice in the matter." He sat down.

Blake stood above him, his arms folded across the expanse of his chest, his biceps bulging. "You wanted to know Autumn's involvement in all this?"

He shrugged. "Sure."

"The man I work for, General Dumas, wants to figure out a way of turning regular humans into spirit shifters. He wants to use them to create an army which will have an advantage above all others."

Chogan's mouth fell open. "You have got to be shitting me."

Blake scowled. "Are you going to let me talk?"

His cousin fell silent.

"Autumn, Doctor Anderson, was brought in to try to replicate how a shifter's genetics change when we shift, and she was trying to do so with human DNA."

Chogan shot her a look and she shrugged in an apology. "I didn't know what I was working with then, only that I'd never seen it before."

"Anyway," Blake interrupted, "while she was conducting her experiments, she cut her finger and some of her blood contaminated the slides. The human DNA began to change, just like shifter DNA."

"You're telling me she's able to change humans into shifters?"

"There's a possibility, yes."

She held up her hands. "We don't know that yet. I wasn't able to confirm the experiments properly. Your cousin here got me out of there quicker than I had time to think."

"We had no choice. If Dumas had of gotten there before me or Haverly, you'd be locked up beneath ground right now. You were lucky Haverly was with you when the accident happened."

A thrumming from above their heads caught everyone's attention, causing them to simultaneously lift their faces to the ceiling. The sound grew louder, a pulsing on their ears.

"What the hell?" Blake went to the window and peered out, before turning on Chogan. "Did anyone see you? Follow you back?"

Chogan frowned. "I don't think so. There were a lot of people around."

"Well an unmarked chopper is right above the hotel. I'm going to guess it isn't just sightseeing."

"Shit."

Autumn turned from one man to the other. "What's happening?"

Blake picked up his leather jacket and threw Autumn her coat. She snagged the item from the air and pulled it on, though the thin suit jacket wouldn't offer much protection in the cool evening.

"Dumas must have had people positioned outside the building to watch out for anything unusual. I'm guessing Chogan's appearance fell into that category and they've sent someone after him, hoping to find us. We need to get out of here." His hand made contact with her lower back, hustling her out of the room. "Let's go!"

Though frightened, she couldn't deny the thrill she experienced at the sensation of his big, hot palm pressed so close to her skin. The memory of the kiss they'd shared was still at the forefront of her mind.

Together, they ran down the corridor. The sound of the helicopter grew louder, the roar quickly developing into a *thwop-thwop-thwop* which pounded on their ear drums.

A window was positioned at the end of the corridor. The previous view of the city was blocked as the aircraft appeared, hovering just outside. The interior of the helicopter was open to the air. Autumn caught a glimpse of a man in protective gear crouched inside its body, something held between his hands, before the window exploded inward and her senses were overloaded by the shatter of glass and a rattle of automatic gun fire.

She dived for the floor, helped in part by Blake shoving her down from behind. The cheap hotel carpet was suddenly far closer than she'd ever anticipated coming to it, the garish colors and pattern vivid in her vision as she crawled, commando style, to reach the nearest exit.

"Go!" Blake shouted.

Chogan was already ahead and he turned to reach out to her, grabbing her hand so they rose to a crouch together and scuttled toward the fire door.

Blake pulled his weapon and fired off three shots in succession through the hole where the window had been only moments before.

"Blake!"

Terrified for him, she glanced back to make sure he was following. He fired off another shot before spinning toward them and chasing them out into the stairwell.

They ran down, Autumn's heart pounding. Her feet felt like they couldn't move fast enough, simultaneously wanting to get out of there, while worrying she was going to stumble and pitch headfirst down the stairs. After the deafening roar of the helicopter, the shattering glass and machine gun fire, the slap of their feet against the treads sounded strangely hollow.

Movement came from below, the sound of people running up the stairs toward them.

"Shit!"

Blake's fingers wrapped around her wrist and he yanked her away from the stairwell and through another door. He pushed her out onto another floor, hustling Chogan along with her. The Hispanic woman who'd passed them earlier stood frozen in the action of letting herself into a room on the second floor. From her upturned face and wide eyes, she'd obviously noticed the commotion from above.

Without pausing, Blake pushed past her, dragging Autumn with him, Chogan following close behind. He ran to the window and opened it, leaning out above the alleyway below. On the opposite side of the alley stood an industrial trashcan filled with black trash bags.

"You're going to have to jump."

"What?" She stared at him in alarm.

But Chogan was already climbing onto the ledge. "Don't worry, I'll catch you." Cat-like, he sprang from the ledge, landing with a flurry of trash in the can. His head popped back up and he held out his arms to her. "Come on," he yelled up, his fingers beckoning her toward him.

"Do it now!" Blake insisted, peering over his shoulder, his gun still clutched in one hand and pointed toward the hotel room door.

"You have got to be kidding me," she muttered. She climbed onto the ledge, trying not to look at the drop below. Even though they were only on the second floor, the height was frightening from up here. Her legs trembled beneath her and she closed her eyes briefly, willing herself to be brave. She took a breath, gritted her teeth, and leapt.

Autumn fell through the air… and straight into Chogan's arms. He caught her and they rolled together so she found herself tangled in his limbs, pressed against his body. He reached out and pushed her hair from her face, her breath catching as he focused his almost-black eyes on hers.

What's happening to me? These men had a way of capturing her attention.

"Come on." He helped her climb from the can. Moments later, another gunshot rang out.

"Blake!" she cried.

But he dropped from the window, landing on his feet in a crouch on the ground.

"Well, what are you waiting for?"

They ran, putting distance between themselves and the hotel. They stayed close to the walls, keeping out of sight of the chopper above. Quickly getting lost in the bustle of the city, they left the helicopter and the men chasing them far behind.

AUTUMN STOPPED AND bent over, her hands placed on her knees as she gasped for breath, her lungs burning. She tried to speak, but the effort only rasped her throat, making her cough. Annoyingly, the two men seemed relatively unaffected by the long run. At least she hadn't been totally out of shape and unable to run at all. She couldn't imagine how embarrassing that would have been. She'd often been jealous of her roommate Mia's small, curvy frame, but for once she was thankful for her own tall, athletic figure. Plus, the running she liked to do when she was trying to figure out a problem had also helped.

She managed to catch her breath enough to speak. "Where the hell are we going?" So far, they'd been heading out of the city, and now only the occasional house broke up the street. They'd either have to find a car and get onto the freeway to get away from the city, or else head into the miles of forests and State Parks which stretched out for thousands of miles either side of the city.

The two men exchanged a glance.

"I only know of one place where we might be safe," said Chogan.

Blake's lips thinned to a line. "Oh, no. I'm not going back there."

"Where?" she asked, looking between them.

"He's talking about going back to the reservation."

"People there will be able to help us," Chogan insisted. "They'll understand."

"I'm not going back."

Chogan grabbed Autumn's arm. "Fine, but I'm taking her with me."

Autumn laughed in surprise, though her reaction wasn't due to humor. "Err, I don't think so! I go where I want, not where I get taken."

Chogan let go and folded his arms. He looked at her from beneath his dark brows. "Fine. Ask him if he's got any better plans. Both of you have your faces plastered all over the news. If you stay in public, these people who are after you will find you."

"If you hadn't gone near the government building, they'd never have found us anyway," she snapped.

"Yeah? Don't you think someone would have reported you eventually, like that chambermaid?"

Autumn remembered the woman passing them in the corridor, and then again when they'd been searching for an escape. Chogan was right, and after all the commotion at the hotel, they'd be more visible than ever. "Perhaps Chogan is right," she said.

Blake reared back as if she'd slapped him. "What? You're taking his side?"

"I didn't realize we had sides here. I thought we were all on the same team."

Chogan offered her a smile, but she didn't miss the way his gaze darted, self-satisfied, over to Blake. "Do you have any other ideas, Cuz?"

"We'll head into the forest, but if there's any sign of anyone following us, we don't go near the reservation. I won't bring these assholes into innocent peoples' lives."

Chogan's face lit up. "So does that mean we'll shift?"

"We'll be faster as wolves, and, of course, they'll never be able to track us."

"But what about the girl?"

Autumn bristled at the word *girl*.

Blake glanced over at her and she felt his eyes travel across her body. Unconsciously, she found herself standing taller, sucking in her stomach. "She'll have to ride."

All the air exploded from her lungs. "Ride? What do you mean, 'ride?'"

"Exactly what I said. I'm plenty big enough to carry you on my back when I'm in wolf form." A smile touched his lips. "I think I'm big enough to carry you when I'm a man as well."

A blush colored her cheeks, a mixture of fear and excitement coursing through her. He couldn't be serious? She'd witnessed his extraordinary change. Surely she couldn't *ride* on him.

"I should take her," interrupted Chogan. "If she's so important. I'm a lot faster than you."

Blake glared at him. "You're not taking her, even if you *are* faster. I'm the one who's stronger."

"When you two have finished your who's-got-the-most-testosterone competition, I'll tell you who is going to take me. Blake, I've seen you as a wolf; I've known you longer. I trust you."

He bowed his head. "Thank you."

As they walked, the density of the buildings began to thin. Ahead, the trees thickened, leaving the city behind. There was a certain peacefulness about the forest now night had fallen. Moonlight peeped between branches, casting eerie shadows on the forest floor. Small animals rustled in the bushes around them, an owl screeched overhead.

They reached a clearing. "Here?" said Chogan.

Blake nodded. "Yes, this will do. He looked over at Autumn. "Are you ready for this?"

"As I'll ever be."

She stepped back, giving the two men space.

Giving each other a modicum of privacy, the men turned their backs on each other. Chogan pulled his shirt over her head and Autumn realized what was about to happen. *Oh crap. They're both going to get naked.* Her heart rate picked up, her eyes darting between them. Though the night was dark, there was enough moonlight to catch the planes and curves of their bodies. Enough light to be able to compare the two.

Chogan pulled the band from his long hair, allowing the thick, shiny black locks to fall around his face and down his back. His body was smaller than Blake's, his skin a shade darker and without the tattoos, but still with perfectly formed abs, his waist narrowing in to a thick patch of dark hair …

She forced her eyes away, down to the ground, but she couldn't help herself and found her gaze drifting back up. She felt drawn to them, to both of them, and she couldn't not watch this extraordinary thing that was about to happen.

Blake followed suit, tugging his t-shirt up over his head. His tattoos were shadows in the darkness, their sharp edges blurred, but he still looked beautiful.

Chogan shed his shoes and jeans, so he stood naked in the night air. He lowered his head, his back, shoulders, and neck straining. The first crack of bone breaking was like a muffled gunshot in the night, and nearby animals scurried away in a burst of movement.

Blake threw the rest of his clothes away. She saw him close his eyes, and then his head flung back and he howled into the night.

She stepped back, frightened, her hand clutched to her mouth. Was this really happening?

All over Chogan's body, fur began to appear, a different shade than Blake's, though the exact color was difficult to distinguish in the poor light. His limbs jerked in uncomfortable angles, one way and then the other, though the man made no sound.

In contrast, Blake voiced his anguish, roaring and snarling like an animal being attacked. The shapes of both men began to change, their limbs lengthening and growing thicker, their backs stretching. Their shoulders became more prominent, necks extending. But of course it was their faces which changed the most. Where one moment she'd been standing beside two men, both beautiful in their own way, with so many similarities, now two amber-eyed wolves stared back at her.

Blake gave himself a shake, his silver fur rippling around his body. He trotted up to Chogan and the two animals touched noses.

Autumn watched, her breath caught in her chest. Both animals were massive, though Blake was bigger than Chogan by at least six inches all over.

Blake trotted over to where Autumn stood trembling. Slowly, he lowered his body to the ground and lay down. He tossed his head toward his back, and she understood what he wanted.

She forced her legs to move and approached the wolf. In the

background, Chogan stood, his head held high, ears pricked, alert for any sounds or movement around them.

She stood close enough to smell the musky scent of wolf, to feel the heat of his breath against her skin. She reached out and gingerly touched his fur. He was real. This was real.

"Are you sure you want me to do this?"

As an answer, he swung his massive head back around and nosed her in the butt, almost lifting her off her feet. She gave a squeal of surprise, not sure whether to laugh or scream. Taking a deep breath to steady her nerves, she leaned up against his shoulders and leaned across to wrap one arm around his neck. He nosed her again, pushing her up, and she swung one leg over his back, her arms around his neck, her thighs locked behind his huge shoulders. She lay flat, her face pressed against the thick, coarse fur, digging her fingers in, like sinking her hand into warm sand. Where she'd previously been cold and wishing they'd allowed her to pick up her thick overcoat before being hustled from the government building, she no longer felt the chill. Heat radiating from the powerful animal's body warmed her.

Blake got to his feet and she clung on tighter, remembering a few horse riding lessons she'd taken as a child and using her thighs to stop herself from sliding from his back. He leapt forward and took off at a run. She gasped as she seemed to leave her stomach behind her, holding on to his neck for all she was worth, hoping she wasn't hurting him. By scooting herself farther forward on his back, she found she could nestle between his shoulder blades, so reducing her chances of falling.

They ran far and fast, the wind tearing through her hair so it streamed in whipped curls down her back. Blake's fur rippled in the wind. Somewhere up ahead, Chogan led the way, covering mile after mile of forest terrain, leaping over small streams, from boulder to boulder, soaring over fallen tree trunks.

Though she could feel Blake's wolf body heaving beneath her as his lungs labored for breath, there seemed to be no slowing to his stride, as though his speed and strength were endless. On occasion, Chogan slowed and gave a small yip or growl, and then they'd change direction a fraction, something Autumn came to realize was them sensing humans or some other potential threat up ahead.

Though she never would have thought it possible, after a couple of hours, the warmth and galloping motion of the powerful body beneath her lulled her to sleep.

CHAPTER FIFTEEN

MIA WALKED TO the apartment window, pulled back the drape, and peered onto the street below. Night had long since fallen and a light drizzle fell, misting beneath the orange glow of a street lamp. She knew she needed to leave the safety of the apartment and go to the police station to report what had happened in Thatcher Woods, but she couldn't quite bring herself to walk out. She'd been hoping Autumn would come home so she'd be able to run the incident past her and get her thoughts on it, but so far that evening she'd seen no sign of her friend.

It wasn't like Autumn to get home late and not let her know. She knew she wasn't Autumn's mother, but the other woman normally called or texted if she was going to be home late.

She's probably gone out with the cute guy from work.

But her internal reassurances didn't ring true. Autumn didn't exactly go on many dates, and if something like a guy asking her out had happened, Autumn would have texted her at the very least.

Mia chewed on her lower lip and peered out at the street again. Someone stood on the sidewalk, a figure looking up at her window.

She frowned, an uncomfortable crawling sensation creeping over her shoulders. A car swept past, blocking her view of the other side of the sidewalk for a moment. When the vehicle passed by, the person had gone.

The events of earlier that day had left her understandably paranoid. She shook her head at herself. She felt like an old clucky hen sometimes, worrying about other people. Sometimes she felt like she'd completely bypassed her twenties and gone straight into middle age.

That's what happens when you center your whole life on worrying about other people.

The buzzer sounded, making Mia jump.

Autumn! She must have forgotten her key.

She pressed the buzzer, unlocking the main front door. "Hey," she spoke into the little intercom. "I was starting to get worried about you."

No answer came and that same chill worried down her spine. Damn, she should have at least asked who was there. Not just assumed.

Stupid, stupid, stupid!

A gentle tap came at the front door and Mia froze, her heart thumping. Where was her phone? She patted herself down and located the item in the back pocket of her jeans. She would call the cops if needed.

Quietly, she made her way to the door, as if she might somehow still be able to pretend she wasn't in, despite having already spoken through the intercom. It was locked, thank goodness, so at least she didn't need to worry about someone bursting in. She stood on tiptoes and peered through the small circle of the peephole. The distorted figure of a man in a smart suit stood sideways to the door. He had a strong, handsome profile, with short blond hair and square jaw. At least he didn't look like a serial killer.

"Hello?" she called though the painted wood. "Can I help you?"

"Miss Henderson?"

"Yes, who are you?"

The man fished something out of the top pocket of his suit jacket and held it up to his side of the peephole, just close enough so she was able to make out the identification. "My name is Calvin Thorne. I'm with a team of government officials involved with trying to locate your roommate, Doctor Autumn Anderson. I wondered if I could have a few moments of your time?"

Her heart lurched. "Autumn? Why are you looking for Autumn?"

"Please, Miss Henderson. I can't discuss this standing out in the hallway. If I could just ask you a few questions..."

Mia hesitated, chewing a dried piece of skin on her lower lip. The weight of her phone rested in her pocket. If she was unsure of anything, she'd excuse herself to the bathroom and call the cops from there.

She unbolted the door and slowly edged it open. "Okay, come in for a few minutes, but I have to tell you that my boyfriend will be here any moment."

The man seemed to repress a smile. "Oh, sure. I won't take up much more of your time."

She stepped back, allowing him into the apartment. "So what's this about? Why are you trying to find Autumn? She isn't in any kind of trouble, is she?"

"Actually, yes, I'm afraid she is. Have you seen the news lately?"

Mia's unease deepened. "No. I don't watch much television."

"Perhaps you should start." He picked up the remote and turned on the flat screen in the corner of the living room. He flicked through until the news channel came on.

Mia stared at him. Why on earth was this man trying to get her to watch the television? "I don't understand what you're telling me."

"Just wait one moment." He hesitated. "There!"

Her attention flicked to the television just as Autumn's face appeared on screen. Mia's heart dropped out of her stomach, her hand lifting to her mouth as she read the travelling headlines on the screen.

Young scientist kidnapped by rogue security guard.

A man's face replaced Autumn's, serious, dark, striking. He looked like he had Native American heritage. *Was this the same man Autumn had been talking about?*

She remembered the agent still standing in the room with her and turned to him.

"Oh my God. Poor Autumn! Is she okay?"

"We don't know that yet, Miss."

"I can't believe it." Her legs gave way and she sat down heavily on the edge of the couch.

"May I?" asked Calvin, nodding to the seat beside her.

"Yes, of course." She shifted up slightly to make room.

"So I'm sure you understand it is extremely important we locate Autumn. We know she has a father still living in the city. Is there anyone else she might try to contact? A boyfriend or close friend, perhaps?"

Mia shook her head. "No, not really. Autumn doesn't date and I'm her best friend. I'd be the one she'd contact if she could." Her mind was in a whirl. She'd been so preoccupied with the case of Toby West, she struggled to comprehend that her roommate was now the one missing. Why on earth would someone want to take Autumn? Her friend was as harmless as they came. All she did was work.

Something in Mia's head clicked. "Does this have something to do with the new project she was working on?"

The man's gray eyes hardened "What has she told you about her work?"

Mia's heart lurched as she caught sight of something she'd not noticed before.

Flecks of gold in his right eye … Oh God …

The world around her seemed to stop. The only sound in the room was the blood pounding through the veins in her temple. Her phone! She needed to call for help. She lurched to her feet and almost stumbled. "I'm sorry," she managed to say, staggering away from him. "I need to go to the bathroom. This has all been such a shock …"

As she spoke, she turned back to make sure the man wasn't following her.

She gave a small scream of fright. He stood, a gun pointed at her head. "What the hell!"

He motioned with the gun. "You need to come with me."

"What? Why?" She felt detached from the situation, as if she was watching all of this happening to someone else. And the thing she really didn't understand was what connection this man had to both Autumn and Toby.

"Do you really think you should be asking questions with a gun pointed at you? Now, get to your feet and come with me."

"You're not going to hurt me, are you?"

"Only if you do something to make me."

CHAPTER SIXTEEN

THE CHANGE OF motion of the warm, furry body she lay upon woke Autumn. She couldn't believe she'd managed to sleep, and not only that, she'd not fallen off. The wolf's run was so smooth she'd not even been dislodged from between his huge shoulders.

The two wolves drew to a halt. Dawn had arrived, and between the expanse of tree trunks, in the burgeoning light, peeped the start of a small town. Simple, single-story wooden homesteads, with wide open front yards, lined a dirt road. The hour was still early and none of the lights in the homes were on, with the exception of a few porch lights.

Chogan sat down on his haunches. Finally, Autumn was able to make out the color of the wolf's fur—a beautiful russet red which caught the gleam of the early morning sunlight. He turned his big head to take her in, his eyes shining golden yellow.

Blake followed suit, sitting down slowly so she slid down his back, her feet planting on the ground. Her legs were numb and tingly, suffering from pins and needles from riding on Blake's back for so long. Immediately, she felt the loss of his body heat, the bite of the morning air even cooler than Chicago. They must have come farther north, crossed the state line into Wisconsin, or even Minnesota.

Blake swung his head to her and nudged her away, his wet nose pushing into her palm. Those intelligent amber eyes connected with hers, speaking to her without needing to say a word.

They'd arrived at the reservation, and now they needed to change back to men.

Autumn retreated, standing slightly behind a tree. She used the trunk as support for her still weak legs, moss and bark flaking beneath her fingertips.

Her eyes widened as she watched the two wolves. She couldn't imagine a time when she would not find this to be utterly amazing and horrifying all at the same time. The thing happening before her eyes wasn't even supposed to exist—a thing of myths and fairy tales, but she couldn't deny what was right in front of her.

The two wolves moved apart, giving each other some space.

Their bodies tensed, Blake's fur trembled, rippling like water. A low growl issued from deep within his barrel chest and he lowered his head as the roar turned into a howl. The mournful sound travelled miles across the forest. She imagined if anyone in the town heard it, they wouldn't be getting back to sleep that morning.

Before her eyes, they began to shift back, fur melting away to reveal human nut-brown skin. The shape and lengths of their limbs morphed, bones shattering and reforming with agonizing howls of pain from Blake. Chogan seemed to suffer the agony in silence, though Autumn felt sure the process didn't hurt any less.

Their long snouts shrank and flattened to their faces, the jaws full of teeth vanishing. Ears rolled down to become flush with their skulls.

Finally, they stood back up, both men again.

Both naked.

Autumn gulped and averted her eyes. As much as she thought she'd never get used seeing them shift, she also thought the regular bouts of nakedness would not be something she'd become blasé to. Of course, it helped that both men were gorgeous—Blake with his huge bulk of muscle and swirls of tattoos, Chogan leaner, but still cut, with his smooth, darker brown skin and long black hair. She didn't think she'd ever been present with two specimens of more perfect male beauty.

Neither man seemed conscious of their nakedness.

"Welcome to Big Lake Reservation," Chogan said.

She gave an uncertain smile. "Thanks." She turned to Blake. His face was a schooled mask, hiding, she suspected, the myriad of emotions churning through him.

"Wait here," said Chogan to his cousin. "People are used to seeing me in this town, but I think you might cause a bit of a stir."

Especially stark naked! Autumn thought, but didn't say.

Chogan ducked down low and ran between the trees, heading out into the town. He stayed close to the parked cars and garden fences, seeking as much coverage as possible. Whatever Autumn had thought about the no-clothes thing, he obviously realized it wasn't normal behavior to run through the streets as naked as the day he was born. He vanished from view.

"Are you all right?" asked Blake, snatching her attention from his cousin.

She couldn't look at him, heat glowing in her cheeks. "I'm fine," she said, keeping her eyes trailed on the ground. It was one thing taking in the sight of him when his attention was elsewhere. It was something else looking him in the face, full frontal.

"I realize this has been a lot to take in."

"Are you kidding me? I've been chased, shot at, and rode around on a giant wolf. This is just a normal working day for me." She risked lifting her eyes to his.

He cracked a smile. "That's good to hear. I wouldn't have wanted to frighten you."

"Takes a lot more than that," she smiled back. "Where's Chogan gone?"

Blake sat on the ground, leaning back against the tree with one leg propped up, the position covering the particular area that kept catching her eye. She was relieved. At least now she could look at him—appreciate the thick breadth of his muscular thighs, hard stomach, and shoulders without thinking she was about to spontaneously combust. Just about.

"He's gone to get us some clothes. We can hardly walk around town like this."

Autumn pressed her lips together to repress a childish snigger.

A rustle in the undergrowth caught their attention and Chogan reappeared between the trees, clothes bundled in his arms. "Stolen from clotheslines, I'm afraid." He threw a pair of jeans and a t-shirt at Blake.

Blake snatched them out of the air.

He dressed, the items way too small for him—the length too short, almost exposing his stomach, his biceps busting out of the armholes. He couldn't even get the jeans done up, though Autumn certainly appreciated the shape of his ass in the soft denim.

He held his hands out either side of his body. "I look ridiculous. Couldn't you have found anything larger?"

"I wasn't exactly in Bloomindales."

Blake narrowed his eyes in annoyance at his cousin, but put out a hand to Autumn. Surprised, she slipped her small palm into his much larger one.

"Let's do this, then," he said.

She didn't miss the flicker of Chogan's dark eyes down to their connected hands. She hoped he wasn't going to cause any problems there. The last thing she wanted was to come between the two cousins, especially when they already seemed to foster a tenuous relationship.

They ran at a jog down the street together, Blake and Autumn hand in hand, Chogan leading the way. Several blocks later, they passed a small grocery store on the corner and then reached a modest home. Like many of the others, with the exception of a number of trailers, the house was a single-story, white-washed, wooden building. Modest but tidy. Chogan walked up the path, toward the front door. Blake stopped at the gate, hesitating.

Chogan stopped and turned back to him. "Everyone will be pleased to see you, you know."

"Yeah? I doubt that, somehow."

"Just because you gave up on us doesn't mean we gave up on you."

Pain flicked across Blake's strong face.

What had happened? Autumn wondered. *What would make him want to leave his home for such a totally different life?*

Chogan let himself into the house, Blake and Autumn lurking behind.

"Uncle?" Chogan called through the open door.

Movement stirred from the back of the property. "Chogan, is that you?"

Autumn felt Blake stiffen beside her, heard his breath catch. In the short time she'd known him, she'd never seen him nervous or uncomfortable, not even when people shot at them and a helicopter chased them. Right now, tension radiated from him like body heat.

"Yes, Uncle, it's me. I've brought someone to visit."

An older man—in his sixties, Autumn guessed, though his face was lined with grooves and ridges deeper than she would have expected from someone his age— approached Chogan, who still stood in the open doorway.

The man's eyes widened and he stared past his nephew, to where Autumn and Blake still waited a little farther down the path. "Blackened Hawk?"

Autumn couldn't help her surprised glance toward Blake.

He smiled. "Hello, Father."

Tears welled in the older man's eyes and he walked past Chogan, arms outstretched. He reached Blake and enveloped the much bigger man in a bear hug. He let go and stepped away, then reached out and took Blake's cheeks and pulled his son's face down toward him. He stared at him, eyes sparkling with amazement, and planted kisses on both of his cheeks.

"My son. The spirits always told me you'd come back to me again." He looked over his shoulder toward Chogan. "Thank you for bringing my boy back to me."

Blake pulled Autumn toward him. She shifted awkwardly from foot to foot, uncomfortable at being literally dragged into such an intimate moment. "Autumn, let me introduce Lakota Wolfcollar, my father." He turned to the man in question. "Father, this is Doctor Autumn Anderson. She's the reason I'm back."

His father's eyes lit up. Blake must have quickly realized the misunderstanding. "Oh, no. Not like that. We're not together."

Autumn tried to ignore the sinking sensation in her stomach. Did she actually want to mean something more to him? No, of course

not. He was not her type in the slightest. She almost laughed out
loud at the thought. She'd barely dated, never mind had a *type*.

"Whatever reason brought you home to me, I am thankful for
it." Lakota Wolfcollar turned to Autumn and nodded slowly at her.
"So I thank you."

"You're welcome," she said with a shy smile, though she
wondered if he'd think differently after he'd heard their crazy story.

BLAKE TOOK A deep breath. Stepping into this house was like
stepping back in time. Almost ten years had passed since he'd been
back here, and the place didn't look much different. Fading family
photographs in wooden frames that had been in the same positions
years before, still covered the walls. His mother—noticeable among
them because of her pale skin—him sitting on his father's knee, and his
sister, Tala, not much more than a toddler, held in their mother's arms.

His gut clenched. However forgiving his father might be about
him walking out on all of their lives, his sister would not be so
lenient. She'd only been fifteen when he left—already fiery and
strong-willed—and he knew his abandonment had left her bitter.
He'd tried to stay in contact, sent her letters and presents from
wherever in the world he'd been stationed, but if she'd even opened
them, he would have been surprised.

"How is Tala?" he asked.

His father smiled. "Same as ever. She's a qualified nurse now, you know?"

Blake smiled ruefully and shook his head. "No, I didn't. She
never answered any of my letters."

"She took it hard when you left."

"I figured she must have."

"You could have come back to visit us."

He shook his head. "No, I couldn't."

He felt Autumn's eyes on him, a curious glance. But he couldn't
go into that now. Especially not with Chogan sitting in the room
with him. His cousin played a big part in him needing to leave the
reservation. After what happened, he knew he'd not be able to

continue any kind of day-to-day life with his cousin around. He was sure if he'd had to see Chogan every day, the day would have come when he'd snap and kill his cousin. And what would have happened then? A rift in the family that would have never healed.

It had been either him or Chogan.

"So speak to me now. Tell me what's brought my only son home to me after all this time." Then he seemed to remember himself. "But of course, you all must be thirsty. Hungry?" He eyed Blake's ridiculously small clothing. "I assume you came here by wolf."

"Yes. We had no choice."

The older man motioned with his hand toward Chogan. "Go, make some tea and food for our guests." Without a word, Chogan got to his feet and disappeared from the room, heading in the direction of the kitchen.

Lakota leaned in and took both of Blake's hands. How strange how he remembered his father to be such a big man, a man who would pick him up and swing him around. It made him sad to feel his touch, now leathery with older skin, though there was still strength to his hands. His father's hair was much shorter, the gray that had previously only flicked at the temples now spread across eighty percent of his head. The thin-rimmed glasses were also a new addition. His face seemed slimmer, his cheekbones hollowed. Blake hoped he was taking things easy. Lakota Wolfcollar had been Tribal President when Blake had been a boy, but surely he must have retired by now?

Blake's feet were planted on the floor and he looked down at their clasped hands. "I barely know where to start."

"Just start at the beginning, my son. I assume the reason for you being here has to do with the disappearance of the other shifters. The reason we sent Chogan to find you."

He nodded and took a deep breath. "I've been working for the US government, though not quite in the capacity I told you. I've been working kind of off-the-record for a man called General Maxim Dumas. Dumas has somehow got wind of the existence of spirit shifters and has been trying to figure out a way of applying the strengths of a shifter to the normal human population."

"My gods."

"That's not all. Autumn here was brought in to try to replicate the genetics of a shifter in human DNA."

He looked at Autumn and smiled. "A smart one."

She smiled back. "So they keep telling me."

His father chuckled and Blake wanted to kiss her for lightening the tension in the room. He continued, "She discovered something she wasn't expecting. A drop of her blood was able to change human DNA into shifter DNA."

His father turned to her, the expression in his eyes one of awe. "So you're one of them?"

She shifted uncomfortably in her seat. "I'm sorry, what?"

"I wasn't aware any of your kind was still around. You must be from a line of the originals, the people who first created our kind."

Blake frowned. "I didn't know such people existed."

"They don't. Or at least I didn't think they did until now."

"I'm sorry," said Autumn. "But I really have no idea what you're talking about."

Lakota dropped one of his son's hands and reached out to hers, so all three were joined in a circle. He focused on her with intelligent brown eyes. "The story goes that thousands of years ago, people wanted to commune with the spirits. They strove to find ways in which to create a greater connection with the spirit world around us. In the end, a shaman was brought in. He conducted a spell using black magic, which gave certain individuals the ability to give others a gift, or a curse, however you want to look at it. The blood of those individuals gave others the ability to make a permanent connection with a spirit of an animal. Over hundreds of years, the ability of a spirit to connect to a human, so creating a spirit shifter, evolved. The spirits grew stronger and learned how to make their own connection to human souls willing to share their lives. The line of people who had originally been changed through the alteration of their blood could no longer shift themselves, but within their blood they still held the secret to creating those who could."

Autumn stared at him and then lifted her hand, touching her blond curls. "But...look at me. I'm ..." She stumbled awkwardly over her words.

"White?" the older man offered.

Her cheeks flushed. "Yes. I don't have any Native American background, so how can I have this bloodline you're talking of?"

"You're a scientist, is that right?" he asked. Autumn nodded. "Then you must know that it is believed in your scientific world that we all originated from one blood line. White, black, brown, it's all the same. Once upon a time, we were all one people."

"I still just find this so hard to comprehend."

His brown palm covered the back of her hand. "I understand, child. But it is not a matter of you needing to believe. You don't need to try to *believe* what is right in front of your eyes. You simply must accept it."

Chogan appeared in the doorway, carrying a tray of cups and toast—a strange sight to see the powerful, long-haired man doing such normal, homely task.

"Blake hasn't told you the full story yet, Uncle."

Blake lifted his head. "No, I haven't. General Dumas is after Autumn now. He wants her blood and what she can do for himself. Not only that… In the laboratories where Autumn and I worked, Dumas has three shifters captive."

"One of those is from Big Lake Reservation," Chogan added.

The older man nodded slowly, then helped himself to tea, adding milk and sugar. "I'm sorry, where are my manners? Please, how do you take yours?" He addressed Autumn.

"Oh, no, I'll do it." She lifted the pot and poured tea.

"So these men are after us, Father. They know I took Autumn, got her out of the laboratory, and that I betrayed them. I doubt they've figured out that I'm a shifter yet, which is why we came here in wolf form. So they wouldn't be able to track us—they'd be looking for two men and a woman. But we can't hide out here forever. We need to go back and save those other people and try to figure out a way to shut down Dumas and his team for good."

His father nodded. "I understand." He turned to Autumn. "And what about you? What do you want from all of this?"

She looked bewildered. "Nothing. I don't want anything, only to go back to my old life and not be chased around by guys with guns!"

"But what about your gift? You're the first of your line I've ever come across. Don't you want to see what your gift can do?"

"I...I...hadn't really thought about it. I guess, scientifically, it's fascinating to me, but at the same time it scares the hell out of me. I don't want to change people. I don't want to hold any kind of powers. I just want to be me. I want to be able to get up and go to work in the morning without worrying that someone is going to try to shoot me."

Chogan spoke up. "You could make us more prevalent than human kind."

"And why would I want to do that?"

"Because you're more one of us than you are one of them."

She got to her feet. "I don't want to be on any sides!"

Blake reached out and took hold of her hand, pulling her back down beside him, centering her. "It's okay. There aren't human and shifter sides; that's just Chogan's way of thinking." He glared at his cousin.

Chogan lifted his hands in defense. "It isn't just my way of thinking, there are plenty of others. Think how people are going to treat her when news gets out about what she's able to do. Plenty of people will want her to try and change them."

"And plenty of others will want her dead because of it. Most of society views us as something out of a horror story—werewolves, beasts, shape-shifters. That Autumn has the ability to create more of us will only make people want to get rid of her."

"Err...neither of you are making me feel any better here," she said.

Chogan ignored her. "What about your sister, Cuz? How do you think she's going to react?"

The spirits never blessed Tala with the ability to shift, even though the concentration of shifters on the reservation was high compared to the rest of society. Her lack of abilities had eaten into her as a teenager. He'd hoped she'd come to terms with it, but he imagined if she found out about Autumn's ability she would probably be one of the first in line demanding to be turned by Autumn's blood.

CHAPTER SEVENTEEN

LAKOTA WOLFCOLLAR ROSE to his feet. "Speaking of your sister, I think now is a reasonable enough hour to go and let her know you're home. She deserves to find out direct from us, not from word getting around town. You know what the reservation's grapevine can be like."

Blake gave a grim smile. "Yes, I know."

"Afterward, you can rest. I'm sure you must all be exhausted."

At his words, Autumn gave a wide yawn. Blake had been aware that she'd slept part of the way here, her soft body embedded against his fur and muscle, but the brief rest clearly hadn't been enough to stave off her tiredness.

"Where is Tala living now?" Blake asked.

"Not far," said Chogan. "Only a couple of blocks over."

"So you see her often?" He directed the question to both his father and cousin, but Chogan was the one to answer.

"Yes, practically every day."

His heart tightened in his chest. "I don't know how she's going to react to me being back."

Chogan chuckled. "I'm looking forward to seeing it."

They got to their feet. His father gave Blake another appraisal, his eyebrows raised. "On second thought, I think you should change first."

He glanced down at the too-small clothing and a smile tugged at the corner of his mouth. "Yeah, I guess so."

"I kept all your old clothes. Your room is the same as you left it."

He looked to Autumn to make sure she was all right with being left alone for a few minutes. She reached out and squeezed his hand, giving him a nod and smile to tell him she was fine.

Blake headed down the hallway, back to the bedroom where he used to sleep as a boy. He'd left at the age of nineteen, too young to bother to move to another house in town. The first time he'd lived away from home had been hundreds of miles away. His hand traced objects from his childhood—an old stereo which still took tapes, the faded posters on the walls. He could hardly believe his father had kept all of this the same. A pang of guilt seared through him.

What else had he expected? For his father to pack up his stuff and forget he ever existed?

He pulled open the dresser and unfolded a pair of jeans and a t-shirt. Quickly, he stripped, replacing the items he wore with the ones from his teenage years. The clothes were a little snug—he'd bulked out since his teenage years, though he'd been big even back then. Still, they fitted a hell of a lot better than the ones Chogan had stolen from someone's backyard.

He went back out to find everyone standing in the entrance hall, waiting for him. Chogan seemed eager, almost hopping from foot to foot. By contrast, Autumn was pale, dark shadows beneath her aqua blue eyes. She looked exhausted and Blake wished they weren't putting her through another excursion. He'd forgotten she didn't have the extra reserves shifters did.

"You can stay here if you want," he told her. "Get some rest in my room." The idea of having her in his old bed sent a thrill through him.

"No." She smiled. "I want to meet your sister."

Chogan threw back his head and laughed. "You might not be saying that after you meet her."

Blake narrowed his eyes. "Ignore him," he told her.

Together, they left the house and walked down the middle of the street. Autumn stayed close to his side and he automatically put his hand around her waist, allowing her to lean against him. Both he and Chogan tired less easily because of their body's abilities, but he guessed, apart from her so far untapped talents, she was as human as anyone else.

She smiled up at him, grateful. "You keep me warm."

"Oh!" He hadn't realized she'd been cold, just tired. "You should have mentioned something at the house. I would have found you a coat."

She shook her head. "No need. I'm good like this."

A spark warmed his heart and he held her a little closer, so her hip pressed against the top of his thigh, her elbow tucking into his waist, her shoulder beneath his arm. It felt good to move like this, like one person.

They followed his father down the road, taking the first left onto another street. Blake couldn't help but compare the neighborhood to how it had been when he'd left. His father had been working hard to bring the properties up to a good living standard. It was always going to be hard getting people to invest in property they didn't technically own. Tribal laws meant the whole of the reservation was owned by all the people living on it. When everyone owned the land, no one owned the land. The result was that the houses built upon the land were worth a lot less than in non-reservation areas, so loans were hard to come by. Hence the reason for there being so many mobile homes.

Still, the community had obviously done their best to bring up the standard of this area, though he had no idea what the rest of the reservation was like. At least Tala had ended up living here instead of one of the poorer areas.

Blake smiled as he observed the small whitewashed house with the picket fence. So his sister had gone all domesticated on him. It was hard to imagine. He wondered if there was a man in her life and found himself frowning. He had no right to try to play the protective big brother.

They piled up the path, nerves suddenly churning his stomach. His father gave a sharp rap of knuckles on the front door.

A few minutes passed. Chogan stepped forward and knocked, harder this time. A noise came from inside, a muffled shout to wait. The door flung open.

A young woman stood on the doorstep, her jet-black shiny hair hanging down to her waist, her slender body wrapped in a robe of some kind of silky material.

"What the hell's going on?" She looked between Chogan and her father, and then past them. Her dark eyes widened, her neck straining forward as though reducing the gap would help her make sense of what she was seeing. She stepped off the stoop, one hand clutching her father's arm as she went, gently pushing him aside.

"Blackened Hawk?" She shook her head. "No, it can't be. I must be seeing a ghost."

"It's me Tala," he said, stepping forward and breaking the contact with Autumn. "I'm home."

"But ..." She shook her head again, blinking. Only a matter of feet separated them now and she reached out a hand and placed her fingers against Blake's cheek. "It is you."

"Yes." His face broke into a smile. "I'm—"

His words cut off as a sharp crack sounded across the otherwise empty street. A moment later, pain and heat seared his cheek and he realized what had happened. She'd slapped him.

"That's for not being around the last ten years," she spat before turning around and storming back into the house.

She'd left the front door open, and Chogan started to head in. When no one else followed, he turned back to face them. "If she'd not wanted you to come in, she would have slammed the door in your face as well."

Blake and Autumn exchanged a look. She offered him a sympathetic smile, and reached up and gently touched his cheek. "You okay?" she asked him softly.

"I deserved it, and I've had a lot worse." He resisted the urge to capture her fingers in his own and kiss her hand.

"Come on, then," Chogan said, laughter behind his voice. Blake guessed he'd enjoyed seeing Tala slap him. "Can't get much worse."

They piled into the house, Autumn awkwardly lurking behind Blake's huge form. He didn't blame her. He couldn't imagine being dumped into a room with Tala on top of everything else she'd been forced to go though over the past twenty-four hours.

His sister stood in the middle of her small living room, her arms folded, her weight shifted to one side, her foot tapping. She didn't appear much different than when he'd left, except she was taller, her hair longer than before. Anger, so often present when she'd been a teenager, still burned in her eyes. Only perhaps that anger was darker now; he wondered if his disappearance for the past ten years had something to do with that.

"So what are you doing back here?" She glared at him. Her eyes shifted to where Autumn stood. "I suppose *she* has something to do with your return. Are congratulations in order?"

He frowned and glanced back at Autumn and realized what she meant. "Oh, no. Nothing like that. Or at least, we are back because of Autumn, but not in the way you're thinking. This is Doctor Autumn Anderson. She's a colleague."

Autumn stepped forward as if to shake hands with his sister, but Blake put out an arm, keeping her back. Tala had barely looked at her. Instead, her attention remained focused on Blake.

"Oh, right. 'Cause the way you two were cuddled up certainly seemed like something was going on."

Blake suddenly found himself unable to look at Autumn, tension buzzing between them.

"Well, whoever she is, I'm not going to leap into your arms and play the doting baby sister, if that's what you were expecting. I've barely heard a word from you in almost ten years and I've done just fine without you."

Blake frowned. "What are you talking about? I wrote to you all the time, from all over the world, wherever I was stationed."

She snorted. "A few crappy letters. Big deal."

"I wrote you every week, Tala. Even after I realized you were never going to reply."

She shrugged and stared at the floor, her naked toes rubbing at the rug. "Maybe I didn't want letters. Maybe I wanted my big brother."

"I'm sorry. I never thought I'd be away so long. The years kind of got away on me."

She lifted her head, fixing him with her sharp, dark eyes. "So what are you doing back now?"

He shook his head. "It's not something I want you to get involved in. I just wanted you to find out about me being here yourself, not hear it from gossip around town."

She gave a weak smile. "Well, thanks for thinking of me...for once."

"Tala, you know what happened. If I'd stayed, I would have broken apart the family. Is that what you wanted?"

"By leaving, you broke us up anyway."

He nodded, not knowing what to say. She was right.

Chogan stepped in. "Right, well, if the heartwarming family reunion thing is done, I suggest we get some rest."

Blake offered his sister a smile. "I'll catch up with you again later, Tala. Even if you're not happy for me to be home, it's still good to see you."

AS THEY HEADED back to the house, Autumn couldn't shake the residing awkwardness she'd experienced from being in Blake's sister's home. The other woman's welcome was in complete contrast to the one they'd received from Blake's father.

"I'm sorry about Tala," Blake said.

"Don't be." She smiled at him. "I can kind of understand her being pissed."

"Yeah, she's angry with me, but she's always been a bit like that. Even before I left."

Lakota interrupted. "Tala's had a difficult life. She lost her mother as a young child."

"Oh!" She glanced to Blake, realizing, of course, that what happened to Tala had also happened to him.

Lakota continued, "It was always assumed Tala would be wolf too. After Blake started to shift from such a young age, and showed such control, understanding and empathy with his spirit guide, then, not long after, Chogan began to shift and was also wolf, we assumed Tala would have the same talents. We even named her, assuming she would become a spirit shifter. Her name means 'Wolf.' But the years went by and a spirit never made itself known to her. The older a person gets without being able to shift, the less powerful a shifter they become—the less in control of their talents they are. Those who obtain guides very late in life often don't even have the ability to shift, they simply have the wisdom and guidance of their animal guides. So the more Tala grew up, the more frustrated she became."

Autumn frowned. "But I thought becoming a spirit shifter wasn't passed down generation to generation."

He laughed, the sound deep and hearty—that of a much younger man. "It isn't. For example, I have never been blessed with the ability to shift. But that doesn't mean some families won't show a greater propensity for the gift."

"So Tala resented her brother and cousin for being able to do what she wanted."

Lakota nodded. "And not only that, it made her feel like an outsider in her own family. Her mother being white also didn't help. Tala found herself unable to fit in properly anywhere, at home or in the community."

Autumn turned to Blake. "But you didn't feel like that?"

He shrugged. "My focus was always on my spirit guide. I didn't think about anything else growing up except for shifting and running as a wolf. Tala never had that."

"And then you left," she said.

"Yes, and I'm not sure she'll ever forgive me."

.

CHAPTER EIGHTEEN

AUTUMN STEPPED THROUGH the front door of Blake's old home and a wave of tiredness washed over her. Blake looked down at her, a crease of concern between his dark eyebrows.

"You must be exhausted. Why don't you take my old room? I'll sleep on the couch." He looked to his father as if for confirmation.

Lakota nodded. "That's fine. I'll be out all day now, I have work to do. So you have the place to yourself. Time to figure out what your next step is going to be."

"I'll leave you to it as well," said Chogan. "My own bed is calling."

Blake guided Autumn to his old bedroom, the heat of his palm burning against her lower back. She looked around curiously at the small collection of sporting trophies, the posters on the walls, the stack of music tapes in the corner. How strange to be transported into the domain of a boy who was very much a man now, standing beside her. Yet, despite the teenage surroundings, she couldn't help the surge of excitement at being in such close proximity to him again. The bedroom was small, Blake's sheer size filling the majority, dwarfing the small, single bed. She sensed the charge between them, the unspoken words of attraction between two adults, though she knew she should have greater things on her mind. Yet still, all she could seem to focus on was the memory of the smooth, brown skin of Blake's back, the strong curve of his pectorals and biceps. How she wanted him to strip naked once more and allow her to run her hands all over his body, committing every inch of his skin to memory.

Autumn did her best to push the thought away. "I feel bad, you sleeping on the couch when I have your bed."

"It's not my bed anymore."

She gave a small smile and sat on the edge. "How old were you when your mom died?"

He sat down next to her. "I was twelve, but Tala was only seven. Her death hit her harder, I think."

"My mom died when I was a child too, though I was only five. I barely remember her, really."

"I'm sorry to hear that." He turned to her, his dark eyes studying her face. "Not the best thing to have in common, huh?"

"I guess not. Though sometimes it's good to be around people who understand a part of your life, a part others have no idea how to empathize with."

"Yeah, I guess that's true."

Blake stood, the mattress lifting with the removal of his weight, and Autumn's heart dipped. What did she need to do to make him understand what she wanted? He'd kissed her once before. She didn't think she was imaging that invisible pull between them that made her think he wanted to repeat the moment. Blake crossed the room and pulled down the blind for her, darkening the room from the strengthening sunlight outside.

"I'd better get some sleep," she said, making sure his attention was drawn back to her.

Knowing his eyes were on her, she stood, shrugging off her suit jacket and dropping the item to the floor. She deliberately unbuttoned her suit pants and wiggled them from her hips, leaving her long legs naked. She sensed him catch his breath, his gaze fixed on her movements. Did she dare remove her shirt? No, she wanted him to want to stay with her, but she didn't want him to think she was some sort of easy lay.

Autumn climbed beneath the sheets, but didn't lie down. Instead, she sat up, her knees pulled into her chest.

Blake glanced away, clearly aware of the tension between them, but unsure of the right move to make. Damn, this guy was frustrating. Couldn't he take a hint?

She reached a hand out to him. "Come here."

His eyes widened.

"I'm still cold."

A smile played on his lips. "Oh, right. I'd better stay for a moment then, until you warm up."

"That would be good. Thank you."

He kicked off his shoes. As he climbed fully-clothed into the small single bed with her, she turned her back to him. She took hold of his big hand, placed it over her hip, and wriggled down the bed.

She tugged him down, pulling his body to fit against hers. He wrapped his arms around her waist, the curve of her back and bottom fitting snugly against him.

"Are you still cold?" he asked her, his voice hoarse.

She smiled in the dim light. "Not anymore."

But he made no attempt to leave, and she didn't want him to.

His heat burned through the material of her shirt. He was a solid block of muscle, rock hard against her softness. His hand lay on the mattress, curled into her, his bicep fitting into the dip of her waist. The heat of his breath gusted against the top of her head. At five-feet-eight, she didn't normally feel tiny and fragile, but here, lying in his arms, she did.

She reached down and took his hand. Brazenly, she pulled it toward her and placed his palm on the swell of her breast. Instantly, her nipple tightened and crinkled beneath the lace of her bra.

Blake stiffened. "What are you doing, Autumn?" he asked, a warning tone to his voice.

"What I've been thinking of doing pretty much since the moment I met you."

She squeezed the back of his hand, forcing him to clutch her harder. She knew he wanted this too. When she pushed back on him, grinding her bottom into his crotch, she could feel his need pressing against her lower back.

But that didn't stop the nerves racing through her. A long time had passed since she'd been with a man—the last time had been a one-night stand she'd immediately regretted, and that had been over a year ago now. But she wouldn't regret this. This wasn't just some guy she'd met. Blake was special—strong, tough, and unbelievably sexy. She wanted to get her hands all over his naked body, had wanted to touch him in that way ever since he'd stripped in front of her in the apartment in the city.

Autumn twisted in his arms to face him. "Tell me you don't want me," she said.

He stared into her eyes, his gaze dark and smoldering. His breath touched her lips, their mouths only inches apart. She didn't know if it had been the events of the past twenty-four hours or if she simply had lost control of her own desires, but she couldn't hold herself back anymore.

"I can't," he said.

She leaned in and kissed him, tentative at first, but then a low growl came from deep inside his chest and he flipped her over, his body held over hers. She reached up and tugged his shirt over his head, marveling in the size of his muscles, the tone of his skin. He lowered his mouth to hers again. This time, the tenderness was gone. He kissed her hard, their tongues tangling in exploration of each other's mouths. Autumn reached up and wrapped her arms around his neck, hooking her feet over the backs of his calves in order to close the gap between them.

Her hands ran over the muscles of his back, their hard planes and curves, feeling them working as she reveled in the touch of his skin and the pleasure of his mouth. He left her lips, kissing down her jaw, her throat. Propping himself up, he feverishly worked the buttons of her shirt before ripping the final two away, sending them flying. Then he tore the material from her body, leaving her in only her bra and panties.

Blake kissed her neck, her shoulders, slipping the straps of her bra from her shoulders, and then the lacy cups from her breasts.

His lips enclosed her nipple and she cried out loud. The searing heat of his mouth was like nothing she'd ever felt before on such sensitive skin, the heat bordering the threshold of pleasure and pain. Blake worked his way down her body, peppering her body in tiny, bite-like kisses, nipping her skin with his lips. He paused at the waistband of her panties and she squirmed beneath him, wanting his lips and tongue on her, wanting to absorb his heat—

The ringing of a phone in the room made them both pause and turn toward the sound, startled.

For a moment, Autumn struggled to place the ringtone, but then she recognized her cell. She frowned in confusion. How had her cell phone gotten here?

She sat up, regretfully pulling her body out from under Blake's caresses.

Sitting back on his haunches, Blake frowned. "How is there a phone in here? I'm pretty sure my father doesn't even own a phone."

She crawled out from under him, planting her feet on the cold floor. Her emotions were torn in two different ways. Part of her wanted to clamp her hands over her ears and tell Blake to continue where he'd left off, but the other part of her had to know who was calling. She'd been sure she'd left her phone in the lab back at the facility, with her purse and work bag. She must have slipped it into her jacket pocket at some point. With all the excitement going on, she'd not even noticed it as she had the latest model smartphone and its weight was minimal.

"It's my phone. I totally forgot about it!"

"What?" His face darkened with anger, but Autumn didn't have time to process his reaction. She needed to know who was calling her. After what she'd seen on the television, she could only guess her father or Mia was trying to get hold of her.

Autumn pulled the phone from her pocket and checked the small display screen. *Number Withheld.*

Not allowing herself to time to think, she hit 'answer.'

"Autumn?" Mia's voice came down the line, strained and high-pitched, as though she was trying not to cry.

"Mia? It's okay, I'm safe. No one's kidnapped me."

"No, you don't understand. A man came to the apartment, Autumn. He threatened me ..."

"What!"

"He brought me to this place. I don't know where I am but—"

Her words were cut off and she heard Mia cry out, followed by a shuffling and scraping noise.

"Mia!" Autumn yelled into the phone. "Mia, are you there?"

A male voice replaced her roommate's terrified one. "Doctor Anderson, I assume?"

"What the hell have you done with Mia? Put her back on the phone right now!"

The man laughed, and Autumn balled up the fist not holding the phone. If he was standing in front of her right now, she'd happily punch him in the face.

"I'm not going to do that, Doctor. I think between you and the ball of muscle I assume is still with you, you can probably figure out where she is. Now, why don't you get your pretty little face back here so we can sit down and talk about this like adults."

Blake leapt to his feet, glaring at her. "Put down the goddamned phone!"

She stared back and shook her head, trying to motion toward the cell. Couldn't he see how important this call was?

Blake reached out, snatched the cell from her hand, and threw it to the ground. He lifted his foot, and, with the back of his naked heel, stomped on the cell, shattering it into several pieces. A sharp piece of plastic cut his foot, blood smearing the carpet.

"What the hell do you think are you doing?" She suddenly found angry tears threatening. "Those bastards have Mia and you've smashed up the only thing I've got to be able to get in touch with her again."

"Goddamn it, Autumn! Think for a moment. If they were able to trace my phone back to my apartment, there is no reason why they couldn't have yours traced as well."

She shook her head. "No! When would they have been able to do that? I've only been at the center for a few days."

"Any time. All they'd need to do is hack into your phone account. They'd only need it for a few minutes."

She remembered the x-ray scanner breaking down as she'd entered the building. Had they taken her phone from her then? Done whatever it was they needed to do to make the cell traceable. They could easily have slipped the phone back into her jacket pocket at some point during the day.

"I don't care. We need to leave right away. I need to get back to help Mia."

He grabbed her forcefully by the arm, holding her body only inches from his. He was still bare-chested, Autumn just in her underwear, which she'd tugged back over to cover her breasts as soon as the phone had rung.

"You're not going anywhere. This is exactly what they want you to do."

She wrenched her arm back and glared at him. "Why would they need to kidnap Mia if they can track me by my phone?"

He frowned. "I'm not sure. Perhaps your roommate has something to do with this as well."

"Mia? She runs a missing person's charity. She's about as un-military as you can get. In fact, the government has even pulled her funding for next year."

Blake arched his eyebrows. "And you don't think that's a coincidence? Don't you think the people Dumas and his lot have been holding captive—even down to the scientist before you—would be considered missing people? Maybe she started asking questions of the wrong ones?"

Autumn shook her head. "No. She's in this because of me and I need to go help her." She spun away from him, gathering her clothes, tugging her shirt on over her shoulders and pulling on her pants.

Blake placed his large body in front of the bedroom door. "I won't let you go."

She stared at him, incredulous. "You won't *let* me? Since when do I need your permission to do anything?"

"Haverly put me in charge of your security. It's my job."

She gestured toward the rumpled bed. "And that? Was that your job too?"

His face betrayed no emotion, a hard mask falling down over his features. "It doesn't matter what you say to me. I'm not going to let you go racing off to save your friend, only to get yourself captured. You're too important to the security of my kind."

"Is that all I am? Only important to keeping your lot a secret?" Her gaze flicked to the window.

"Don't even think about it," he said. "If you go for the window, I'll be forced to find some rope and tie you down to the bed. And don't think for a minute that I'm bluffing."

Hot tears burned the backs of her eyes, and to her own fury and frustration, a single tear spilled from the rim of her eye and trickled down her cheek. Angrily, she turned from him, not wanting him to see, and wiped it away.

"So what do you suggest we do?" she said, her voice choked. "If you think they've traced my phone, we won't have much time."

"No, we don't. I need to contact some other shifters, ask for their help. But we will go and help your friend, just like we'll help the others, I promise."

Autumn pressed her lips together. "Just so you know, I don't do well with this macho bullshit."

His head tilted to one side, one eyebrow cocked. "Yeah, well, just so you know, you *forgetting* about your cell phone may have put this whole town in danger, so quit the girly whining and think about the bigger picture."

He snatched his shirt from the floor, turned and walked from the room, leaving Autumn shocked and breathless. Her legs went weak and she sat back on the edge of the bed. She wanted to chase after him, or else do exactly what she'd been planning as soon as she got Mia's call and get the hell back to Chicago, but his words rang in her ears.

She curled up on the bed, still warm from Blake's body heat and smelling faintly of him, and succumbed to tears. Eventually, exhaustion claimed her.

CHAPTER NINETEEN

CHOGAN PAUSED OUTSIDE the bedroom door.

His cousin was charging around town with all the subtlety of a bull. The man was clearly on a mission. Though Chogan knew he should be offering to help, he couldn't resist taking some kind of advantage, knowing Autumn would now be alone. If his cousin and uncle's story was right and her blood could change regular people into spirit shifters, he didn't intend to let her get too far out of his control. Her being tall, blonde, and beautiful also helped spark his interest, but he'd been there before with Blake and a woman, and he didn't intend to repeat that particular part of their lives again.

He lifted his hand and gently rapped his knuckles on the wood. In the back of his mind, his wolf prowled, edging him on, trying to urge him to send it in first to observe her unnoticed. Only his desire not to encroach on her privacy held him back. From the deepness of her breath, he assumed she was sleeping as planned, but from the state Blake had been in, he thought something else had happened.

He ran a hand through his long hair, pushing it away from his face, and then knocked again. The temptation to walk right in lingered. Why did he care about her opinion anyway?

A choked sound came through the closed door.

He frowned. "Autumn?"

Screw it. He pushed open the door to find her starting to sit up. Her eyes were bloodshot and puffy. Her skin looked blotchy, her mouth bruised and swollen. Strands of her hair stuck to her face, making her appear both vulnerable and sexy. He noticed a couple of buttons of her shirt were missing, a tantalizing hint of creamy skin peeking through the gap.

"Autumn?" he said again, frowning. "What's happened? What's wrong?"

She blinked at him and shook her head slightly as if she'd been expecting to find someone else standing at the door.

She was expecting someone else, you fool. She was expecting Blake.

"Chogan?" The frown on her face matched his own. "Where's Blake?"

"He's off rounding up the forces."

"To save Mia?"

"Who is Mia?"

She looked into his face, and, to his horror, burst into tears. "How the hell has this happened?" She buried her face in her hands. "A couple of days ago, I was worried about a job interview and whether my dad gave a shit about me or not. Now, my best friend has been kidnapped by a bunch of government crazies, and I've discovered people can turn into goddamn animals."

She lifted her head and tossed back her hair, blinking back the tears. "I must be dreaming all of this, or else I've lost my mind and should be sitting in a padded white room right now."

He dropped to his knees in front of her and took her hands. She lifted her eyes to him, pools of ocean blue. "Autumn, this is all real. I'm sorry about what's happened to your friend, but they've taken plenty of our friends as well. She might just end up being another casualty."

She snatched back her hands. "Don't say that!"

"I'm sorry, but we're up against the big boys here. We're bound to take casualties. Even with Blake rounding up help, there's a chance we'll all go down."

She stared at him, alarmed. "What are you saying?"

"I don't think a group of shifters is going to be able to take on a military building and men with guns. There's a good chance we'll go to try to rescue our people only to end up dead as well."

"So why are you going?"

His jaw stiffened. "What else am I supposed to do? Stand by and let them get away with this? As shifters, we're connected to something higher than regular humans. Humans keeping shifters captive is like a twist on what's natural. We should be above them. We should be the ones taking them prisoner, not the other way around. Humans should fear and revere us. We shouldn't be hiding away like dirty little secrets. Autumn, if you are what my uncle says you are—the start of our kind—then, do you understand how special that makes you?"

She closed her eyes briefly and shook her head.

He continued, "You're like the daughter of our maker, the closest thing to having a goddess on earth."

The air seemed to shiver between them and he reached out, intent on touching the smooth skin of her cheek, his hair falling in a sheet like a curtain shielding them from the rest of the world.

Suddenly, Chogan became aware of another presence in the room. In his head, his wolf growled, only to be met with the snarl of another wolf.

"I hope I haven't interrupted anything." Blake's voice came, low, controlled, but with fury bubbling behind his words.

Autumn leapt away as though a ring of electricity had suddenly formed around Chogan's body, propelling her from him.

"Blake!" she cried.

But he ignored her, all his attention focused on his cousin. He stormed into the small room, the two big men crowding the small space.

"So are we back to this again?" Blake said. "You and I after the same girl?"

"Blake!" Autumn said, sounding angry herself now. "You don't have any claim on me, and we weren't even doing anything!"

"It's okay, Autumn," Chogan said. "This isn't just about you."

She lifted both hands and shook her head, stepping back. *Sort it out between yourselves, then,* her gesture said.

Chogan put out his hand and caught Blake's arm. "I wasn't fucking Shian, Cuz."

Blake shook him off, anger blazing in his eyes. "No? Then what were you doing with her out in the forest that day?"

"We were just talking. You know, tea and sympathy, and all that."

"Bullshit! You don't do 'just talking.'

"Shian was my friend as well, Blake. You forget that. Her dying left me just as cut up as you. Don't you think I wish I'd been able to save her that day? I ran those events over and over in my head, trying to figure out if I could have done something differently. One minute we were walking, and the next she'd slipped and hit her head. The doctors said the aneurysm had already formed and would have ruptured at some point. The accident simply sped things up."

"I know all that," Blake growled. "But what I still don't understand is what you were doing with her at all. She was my girlfriend, Chogan, had been since we were not much more than children. She told me she was going to lunch with some friends. She lied to me to spend time with you. Tell me why she'd do that if there was nothing going on between you?"

"I don't have anything else to tell you."

"You're a goddamned liar, cousin. And everyone wondered why I couldn't stomach living in the same town as you."

Blake caught sight of Autumn. "I'm sorry you had to be a part of this. Now you're welcome to him."

"Hang on a minute!" Chogan reached out and grabbed him.

Blake lashed back around, his face a sneer.

His eyes flashed yellow…

AUTUMN GASPED AND backed against the wall supporting the bed's headboard.

Blake's snarl made her jump. His eyes flashed that burning yellow she had seen as a wolf, and he suddenly hunched over, a low roar emitting from his chest.

Her eyes flicked to Chogan.

"Don't do this, Cuz," the other man warned, but the warning came too late. The change had already started.

Chogan's face whipped toward her and she saw the same amber color in his dark eyes. He opened his mouth to speak, but long, sharp teeth already filled his mouth, his jaw beginning to elongate. "Go," he managed to tell her, his words mumbled, like he had a mouthful of cotton. "Run!"

She darted one way, but Blake's changing form already blocked the door to the room. She tried to move toward the window, but now Chogan filled that space, his body in the throes of the shift. Unlike before, when they'd both removed their clothing, now their shirts ripped with their changing bodies, jeans left in tatters.

"Stop it, both of you!" she demanded, but they didn't even hear her.

Blake lifted his now almost fully-wolf head and howled, a mournful, heartbreaking sound that seemed to echo right inside her head. Autumn clamped her hands to her ears, thinking her eardrums might burst from the vibrations. He shook his coat, the final remains of his clothing falling from his body. She caught sight of Chogan, his beautiful russet coat now complete.

The big, silver wolf that had been Blake lowered his chest to the floor, like a cat after a mouse, and pounced.

In a twisted, snarling bundle of fur and teeth, the two wolves fought, crashing over everything they came into contact with. The stack of tapes exploded, plastic shattering. The small collection of sports trophies crashed to the floor.

Autumn screamed, pressing her back tight to the wall, her heart in her throat.

The two wolves separated, circling each other as best they could in the limited space. Chogan's massive shoulder brushed by her, the fur soft and warm, a total contrast to the fierce terror she experienced at the sight of them.

Both wolves crouched and sprang at each other again, meeting in midair. They hit with a clash of teeth and claws. With Blake being the stronger wolf, he forced the other wolf to land on its back, crushing a bookshelf beneath their combined weight. Autumn gave another shriek of fear, and Blake spun around to face her.

Blake's amber eyes locked on Autumn, and a shiver of terror trembled through her. Would he attack her? Would he even know who she was, or had his wolf completely taken over? She didn't know how much of him still existed in there.

"Blake?" Tentatively, she reached out a hand. Behind him, Chogan paced in the small space, his eyes fixed on the scene unraveling. "Nothing happened between me and Chogan. It's you I want."

There, I've said it out loud. And to a giant wolf at that.

He moved forward, lowering his head. He pressed against her body, his nose nuzzled against her hand, his cheek against her breast, rubbing up against her like a cat. Her hand went up and rubbed the top of his head, traveling over to run the tips of his ears, like slips of velvet, between her fingertips.

Above his head, her eyes darted toward Chogan. The other wolf didn't look like he wanted to fight, pacing, alert, but not attacking.

Blake stepped away from her and sat back on his haunches. A shudder went through him and he whimpered as the change began, the whimper morphing into a howl. She winced as bones cracked and reformed, as his fur melted back to skin and his eyes became human once more. Blake rose from a crouch. This time she couldn't feel anything except empathy for him, no reaction to his nudity. His vulnerability for such a strong man caught at her heart. He'd loved someone and lost her; that much was clear. She now knew the reason for his abandonment of his home, for the pain she saw in his eyes when he spoke of his past, and the reason for his antagonism toward his cousin. Not only did he blame Chogan for his girlfriend's death, but he also thought Chogan had been playing behind his back. No wonder he'd reacted so badly to seeing his cousin and her in such an intimate position before.

Suddenly, nothing seemed more important than making him understand how she felt. Though she'd not quite figured out her own emotions in her mind, she knew in her heart that the most vital part of her life suddenly focused around him being in it.

Behind them, Chogan, too, changed back to a man. She couldn't help her eyes being drawn to the sight. Would the change ever seem real, or would she forever feel like she was watching it happen on the television, complete with special effects?

Chogan grabbed some clothes from the dresser and pulled them on, both the shirt and jeans hanging from his frame even though he was a big man himself.

Blake reached out and took her hand. She wanted to step toward him, to close the gap between their bodies and lay her head against his chest, feel his heartbeat, but something held her back.

"I'm sorry," he told her. "I didn't want to get you involved in all of this."

"I meant what I said."

He shook his head. "I can't do this again. I've been here before and it split my life in two. I can't put my heart through that sort of pain again. Perhaps Chogan would be the best man for you. At least he knows what he wants."

Chogan wanted her? Was that what he was saying?

She glanced at the other man, but Chogan's face was unreadable, not making eye contact with either of them, his attention fixed at some spot on the floor. She didn't know how she felt about the idea of the other man being interested in her. She couldn't deny he was attractive, and sometimes even gentle, but he had something else about him—a hard edge Blake didn't have—that made her uninterested.

"I'm not forcing you into anything," she said, finally. "I certainly don't want to come between you and your cousin. There's obviously history between you which has nothing to do with me."

"And I want to keep things so it has nothing to do with you. We have enough to worry about without dragging the past into our present."

A knock at the front door drew their attention.

"I'll get it," said Chogan, now fully clothed. He didn't look at either of them as he bustled past, leaving the room.

Blake pulled open a dresser drawer to retrieve more clothes. Her eyes skimmed his back, the hard curve of his buttocks, the strong thighs, the sculpted shoulders, and her heart ached. Had she ever wanted someone so badly? She didn't want to believe that he didn't want her, too, and a part of her didn't. He was only trying to protect his heart from a past pain.

Voices came from down the hall—a man's voice, joined by another, and another.

"They've arrived," Blake said, pulling on a t-shirt and fastening a new pair of jeans.

Autumn frowned. "Who has?" If the voices had been angry, she'd have assumed Dumas' men had arrived, but they sounded more urgent and serious than threatening.

"The people who are going to help us."

CHAPTER TWENTY

BLAKE HEADED OUT to the living room, Autumn following close behind. A small group of people had gathered in the space, perched upon the armrests of the couches, leaning against the walls, a couple of women even sitting on the floor.

He looked across the small group of men and women, and noted the presence of his father, standing in the corner. His presence reassured Blake, though he was surprised not to see Tala here. Even though he'd deliberately avoided her house—his sister wasn't a shifter—she had a nose for trouble and would realize something was going down.

He took a breath and began. "I expect you're all curious as to why I've asked you here."

"No shit," one of the men called out, a skinny guy in his early thirties. "You've been gone almost ten years and now here you want our help. I feel like kicking you out myself."

"Shut it, Enyeto," one of the women said. "Like you'd be able to kick him out anyway. He's twice your size."

Nervous laughter erupted around the group, and the man, Enyeto, scowled.

Blake took back control. "This isn't about me. As you may or may not know, I've been working for a department of the government linked to the military and defense. A certain man, General Maxim Dumas, somehow learned of our kind and what we are able to do. He decided our skills would be perfect for the military—being able to send troops into battle with the ability to not only see ahead into enemy territory, but also, if injured, healing faster, allowing them to be back on the field within a matter of hours. He's set up his own project, *Operation Pursuit*. You've all heard rumors of spirit shifters going missing; well, I'm afraid in several cases I'm aware of, and probably more I'm not, Dumas is responsible. In fact, I know where several of these shifters are right now, which is why I need your help."

"You know who took them?" another woman said.

"Yes, and now I need your help getting them back."

"How are we supposed to help?" someone else called out.

"The shifters are being held beneath ground in a government facility in Chicago. The building is for research and development, but the levels below ground are being used for research into shifters. Only Dumas and those directly below him have access to this level. I'm one of those people. Some of you I need to use as a distraction to allow me to get access to the shifters without being noticed. The others, the ones who want to fight, I need to come in with me to deal with Dumas."

Enyeto jumped up. "I'm in. I'm not going to let some crooked government official think he can use us!"

Blake smiled. He'd been hoping Enyeto would be in. Despite his size as a human, he could pack a punch when needed.

"Me too." One of the women, in her forties with long, silky black hair got to her feet. "I'll do whatever I need to help get them back."

He gave her a slow nod. The woman's particular skills would also come in handy. "Thank you, Peta."

"Hang on a minute!" another voice called out.

Blake's attention moved to an older man he'd known from his childhood. His heart sank. The man was the uncle of Shian, and he'd never approved of Blake even when Shian had been alive.

"How can we even be sure he's telling the truth? He's been gone for years and suddenly he reappears back here and we're supposed to just follow him? For all we know, he's on the other guy's side, and this is a trap to get us all in one place."

Chogan's voice came from the back of the room. "That's not true, Kanen. I've been with Blake over the last couple of days, during times this man, Dumas, has been trying to kill him. Blake's given us no reason to doubt him."

Blake's father straightened. "I hope you're not trying to say my son is capable of betraying his own kind, Kanen?"

The other man's cheeks blossomed with color, his eyes shifting to the floor. "Well he did walk out on everyone, remember?"

"He did what he thought was best at the time."

Blake didn't want everyone else fighting his battles. "My time away has meant I've been able to monitor these people. If I hadn't done that, none of you would be any the wiser in learning what had happened to the shifters who went missing."

Chogan called out, his voice firm, "Blake is still loyal to us, no matter where he's been."

Blake's gaze shifted to his cousin. Despite his affirmation of Blake's character, the sight of the other man still riled him, especially after he'd walked in on him and Autumn getting up close and personal.

One by one, each of the people stood, voicing their support. Chogan hung out at the back of the room, leaning against the wall, his arms folded. Blake sensed Autumn's presence at his shoulder. Should he tell them about the real reason for Autumn's involvement? No, it would be too dangerous for her. He didn't know how the others would react, and he was pretty sure more than one of them shared Chogan's opinion that their kind should be the ones ruling the world, not the ones hiding in the shadows. But still, he needed to tell them something to explain her presence. They would start asking questions soon enough.

He reached back and wrapped his arm around Autumn's waist. He felt her stiffen beneath his touch before she relaxed and allowed herself to be pulled to his side. The possibility his rejection of her had changed the way she thought of him stirred something dark and uncomfortable inside him. His feelings for her were a mess. He couldn't face allowing himself to fall for someone again, not knowing whether he might lose her.

"I'm sure many of you will be wondering about Autumn here." A low murmur went around the group. "Autumn is a scientist who was working on a project the man I told you about, Dumas, had set up for her. She had no idea what he was up to, and as soon as she found out she ran. Only now, her friend, Mia, has been kidnapped by Dumas and his men. Mia runs a charity for missing people and we think one of those people might have been one of our shifters. She was trying to help us and got caught up in this, so we need to find her as well. Okay?"

A murmur of confirmation rose up.

He felt Chogan's eyes on him, knowing he'd want Blake to tell them the truth about Autumn. Perhaps his cousin would out her himself just to spite him, but if he had his suspicions right, then Chogan would also want to protect Autumn. He didn't think he'd imagined the way his cousin acted around the blonde scientist.

But his cousin remained silent, and so Blake continued.

"General Maxim Dumas is at the core of all this, though I suspect someone higher up is probably pulling his strings. If any of you happen upon him before I do, unless your hand is forced, you're to leave him to me. Is that understood?"

"How will we know when we find him?" Enyeto called.

"You'll know. He'll be the one shouting out orders."

Blake stepped forward and pushed the coffee table to one side, creating a space on the rug. He dropped to his knees. "So here's the plan. We'll reconvene at midnight a couple of blocks from the building."

He drew a map with his finger on the rug, the pressure leaving darkened lines in the pile.

"The roof is flat, with a helipad and a small building where the staircase is housed. This entrance is most likely going to be open. The staff tends to sneak up here for a smoke. We'll take Dumas on from three levels. Those who can shift into birds will be going in from roof level to create an initial distraction. A group on the ground can enter into the main part of the building. I'll be coming up from below through a series of tunnels which run below the street. I have the access codes, assuming Dumas hasn't thought to change them."

"And if he has?"

"Then I'll be forced to make a slightly less discreet entrance. But Dumas wants Autumn and me back in the facility, so I'm relying on the fact that he won't want to do anything to keep us out, including changing access codes."

"So do you plan for us to go in our animal forms?" asked Enyeto.

Blake shook his head. "Not at first. We'll go as men and women, but then we'll change."

"There will be a dangerous point when we're shifting," said Kanen, apparently now onboard, despite his misgivings. "It will leave us all vulnerable."

"That's why we won't be shifting all at once. We'll have someone watch each of our backs until the coast is clear. Our main focus is getting the other shifters out of the building. If I can get them back out through the tunnels without anyone even noticing the breach, then I will. But my secondary focus has to be on finding Dumas and putting an end to what he's doing."

Enyeto frowned. "How are you planning on doing that?"

"It's probably best if you don't know."

An uncomfortable silence fell over the shifters.

Blake cleared his throat. "Right, so we'll reconvene in the city and smooth over the finer details there."

They began to turn to each other, the low murmur of conversation rising to a heated discussion about Dumas and the things he'd done to their people.

Autumn's touch on his arm drew his attention. "Where will you want me in all of this?"

Blake frowned. "Right here."

"What? I'm not going to hang around here while you go in and save the day."

A surge of annoyance welled up inside him and he took hold of her hand, tugging her away from the others and into the kitchen.

"You're not going back to the facility!"

She crossed her arms and narrowed her eyes in a stance he'd come to think of as 'Stubborn Autumn.'

"You need me. They outnumber us four to one, at least. You can use another set of hands. Besides, you wouldn't even recognize Mia. How will you know if you find her?"

He scowled. "I guess I'll just have to ask."

She cocked her eyebrows. "How do you plan on doing that if you're a wolf?"

She had him there.

"Also," she continued. "I have a right to know what it is you plan on doing with Dumas. This involves me just as much as it does you."

"It's best if you don't."

"Well, not that you've asked for my opinion, but it seems to me that the only way to stop Dumas and make it so I'm not looking over my shoulder for the rest of my life is by exposing this whole thing."

"I've told you what will happen if the public finds out about my kind. We'll be thought of as freaks, targeted by those who fear us."

"Okay, but if people find out he's been holding people prisoner and torturing them, I'm going to guess his operation will get shut down pretty damn quick."

"You'll still be exposing the rest of us, plus, there's a chance Dumas will walk free. The government is very good at covering up for their own. If he walks free, he'll come after you. This is his obsession."

"So I guess I have no choice. I have to give up my life and everything I've worked for and live the rest of my life looking over my shoulder, all because of some weird genetic defect in my blood."

"Or we kill him."

Chogan's voice came from the doorway.

Blake turned to his cousin and nodded. "Or we kill him," he said in agreement.

Autumn blanched. "I don't want people killed."

Chogan straightened and walked fully into the room. "Even a psycho who has kidnapped your best friend?"

"It's vigilante justice. I'd rather see him go through the courts for what he's done."

"That's never going to happen," said Blake.

"What about all those people out there?" she said. "They don't seem like people who would kill a man."

"Perhaps as humans they're not, but in their animal forms they are. An animal doesn't consider the things a human does, it only does what it needs to survive. In this situation, their animal guides will show them what to do."

"They'll fight for the cause," said Chogan. "They know what's being done to those shifters is wrong."

Autumn chewed her lower lip. "I hope you're right."

Voices rose from the living room again. Chogan turned and left, Blake watching him go.

"What about you and Chogan?" Autumn asked, keeping her voice low. "Are you two going to be able to put your differences aside?"

"I don't trust Chogan. You know that."

"So cut him out. Leave him behind."

"You don't understand. We need him."

"Just because of our numbers? Surely it's better to have one person less than someone by your side you don't trust."

Blake paused and then said, "You've noticed that when we shift, our fur is a different color."

She nodded. "You're silver and Chogan is a russet red. I thought, because your hair is black, your fur would be too."

He shook his head. "The color we are as a wolf isn't anything do with us. It's to do with the type of guide our spirits are. Each color has a different strength. For example, my silver fur means I am a protector."

A small smile played on her lips and she lifted her eyes to his. "I could have guessed that."

He smiled back and glanced away briefly before looking back at her.

"And red?" she asked. "What does red mean?"

Blake frowned. "Fighter. It means Chogan is a fighter."

"So that's why we need him."

Blake nodded.

She seemed to mull this over.

The voices in the living room rose another notch and she looked toward the sound. "I guess you should get back in there before they rile up the whole reservation."

He grinned. "I'm not sure that would be a bad thing."

As they headed back out into the hall, the door burst open. A young man in his early twenties stood in the doorway, his eyes wild. "There's a van full of men in SWAT gear on the outskirts of the reservation!"

The people in the other room all rose to their feet, looking worriedly at each other.

Instantly, Blake focused in on his wolf, trying to get an idea of what lay outside. The big animal ran through the streets, heading toward the edge of the town. A few people had wandered out of their homes, wondering what the disturbance was. The now familiar thrum of helicopter blades filtered through to his sensitive ears.

He and Autumn exchanged a glance.

"Shit!" he said. "They've already found us."

CHAPTER TWENTY-ONE

THE INHABITANTS OF the small house burst into action.

"Quick, everyone, out the back," said Blake. "Head into the forest and shift. They won't be able to track you so easily in animal form."

The shifters grabbed their things, hustling to get out of the property. Too many bodies filled the small space, jostling each other in their haste to get out. Autumn's heart fluttered in fear as she kept her back to the wall, trying to stay out of the way, unsure of what to do.

"We'll meet you in Chicago, Blake," said Enyeto. "We won't let these bastards win."

Blake gave him a grim nod.

Lakota Wolfcollar stood tall. "I'll try to put them off the scent. I'll tell them you were here, but that you left hours ago."

Blake shook his head. "You should hide too, Father. I don't know how far they'll go to get information from you."

Lakota's lips thinned. "No one is chasing me out of my home. This is a reservation. Those men don't have any authority here."

Seeming to remember Autumn, Blake took hold of her arm and shoved her toward Chogan. "Take Autumn. You're faster than me. You need to get her out of here."

Chogan caught her against his strong body, but she spun back to Blake and blurted, "But you don't trust him! You said so yourself."

His eyes flicked coolly toward Chogan. "I guess I don't have any choice in the matter. You need to get out of here."

"No!" she cried. "I won't leave you."

"You have to. Don't worry, I'll catch you up. You need to leave here. Right now."

Tears threatened, her lower lip trembling. "Please, Blake. Don't make me go without you."

"It's all right. I'm trained to deal with these people, and I won't leave the reservation in their hands unprotected. I'll be fine. Now get the hell out of here."

She hesitated again.

"Go!" he snarled at her.

She turned back to Chogan. The other man caught her by the hand and they ran from the rear of the house, across the yard and out onto the street behind. The thrum of the helicopter grew louder and louder. Autumn craned her neck, trying to catch its location, but Chogan yanked on her hand again, pulling her forward. She had to watch where she was going or she'd fall over her own feet. Her breath rasped in her lungs, her heart hammering so hard she thought the organ might burst from her chest. Shouts came from behind them, and they exchanged a wide-eyed glance. Chogan was much faster than she was, but she pushed herself hard, her feet pounding the sidewalk, her thighs burning, determined not to be the one responsible for getting him caught as well.

Oh, Blake…

They left the outskirts of the small town and broke through the line of trees. The terrain was harder going now, her feet seemingly resolute in getting caught in roots or in stumbling over rocks. Whip-like branches lashed at her face, and she used the hand Chogan wasn't holding to shield her eyes. The sound of the chopper faded, replaced by the rustle of wind moving through the trees.

Where had everyone else gone? The reservation and surrounding forest was plenty big enough for them each to get lost in.

A stitch ripped pain in her side. "I'm sorry," she gasped. I need to—" She couldn't finish; there wasn't enough air in her lungs.

Chogan noted the state she was in and stopped beside her, glancing over the top of her back where she was bent double. "We can't stop long."

He seemed to make a decision. He reached beneath his leather jacket and pulled out a gun, handing it to her.

She took the weapon from him, the metal cool and heavy in her grip.

"Where the hell did you get this?"

"Never mind where I got it. Do you know how to use it?"

"I think so." The past forty-eight hours had brought her closer to guns than she'd ever been in her life.

"It's just in case they catch up before I've finished shifting." On the last word, his bones crunched, cracking, his shoulders wrenching one way and the next. His face stretched, teeth appearing in his lengthening jaw.

"Oh God," Autumn whimpered, taking several steps away from him. She held the gun out at arm's length, pointing it in the direction they'd come. She didn't want to have to shoot someone, though she would if it came down to them or her.

Or Chogan. I'd shoot them for Chogan.

But Blake doesn't trust him. Had something really been going on between Chogan and Blake's girlfriend when they'd been younger? From Chogan's disposition, she certainly wouldn't put it past him to have tried something, but she also got the impression that he would be the first to admit it if something had been going on. And despite what Blake said, Chogan did seem to genuinely care about his cousin. It had been such a long time ago now, what reason would he have to continue lying?

Unless he was trying to protect Blake from something …

She realized how close she'd grown to the two cousins in such a short space of time. There was no denying they were special, but she felt more connected to them than she had to anyone else—probably with the exception of Mia—in her whole life.

The big, russet wolf approached, his head lowered in a form of submission. Autumn checked left and right, making sure none of the men now swarming the town was heading toward them. She waited a moment longer, praying Blake would come bursting through the woods, but he didn't appear.

Oh, Blake. Please stay safe.

Feeling like she was leaving a part of herself behind, she turned from the direction of the town and ran to the wolf waiting for her. She checked the safety on the gun and then shoved it in the waistband of her suit pants before stopping beside Chogan.

Before she climbed onto him, she remembered something. "Hang on," she told him.

Running to where he had completed his shift, she scooped up his discarded clothes, bundling them together in her arms. When they reached the city, he would need something to wear.

"Okay, ready," she said, back at his side. He lowered his body down to the ground, allowing her to swing one leg over his back and pull herself on, straddling his back. She stuffed his clothes between her body and his, then leaned forward, placing her bodyweight between his shoulders, burying her fingers into the soft fur of his neck.

Movement came from behind them and she turned to see men appear between the trees.

"Go!" she urged him. "They're coming!"

A shot rang out, a hot streak of air close to her ear. Instinctively, she lay closer to Chogan's back. The wolf leapt forward, taking off at a gallop through the forest.

Blake had been right, Chogan was faster. But then, they'd not had men shooting at them when she'd been riding with Blake. More shots cut through the air, but now they seemed farther away. They were leaving their attackers, and Blake, behind them.

Please be all right, please be all right.

She placed her cheek against Chogan's red fur and was surprised to find it damp. Only then did she realize she was crying.

He continued to run, his powerful body moving beneath her, loping through undergrowth, splashing through rivers, leaping from boulder to boulder. He slowed in places, navigating harder territory, but as soon as they were in any kind of space, he took off at a gallop, the wind tearing at her hair. She buried her face in his fur to escape the force of the air.

They'd been going for a couple of hours now, but he didn't seem to tire. Daylight faded, to be replaced by a purple dusk and, finally, night. The daytime sounds of the forest, tweeting of birds, were replaced by those of night, the scurry of nocturnal animals and the hoot of an owl.

This time, Autumn didn't sleep. She was too worried about Blake, praying the other shots she'd heard hadn't been meant for him, hoping Dumas' men hadn't taken him captive. Would he be waiting for her and the others as planned? She thought her heart would break if they reached the rendezvous point only to find him missing. What would they do then? While she was sure Chogan would try to lead the rest of the shifters in a rescue attempt, she would feel so much better with Blake by her side.

Finally, they slowed to a trot.

They were on the outskirts of the city. Chogan needed to shift back.

She climbed down and moved away. In a small clearing, he sat on his haunches, his body shrouded in moonlight. Bones cracked and snapped into place, his limbs shrinking, fur melting back into his skin. She blinked several times, her brain still trying to convince her that what her eyes were seeing wasn't real.

Chogan stood naked before her, his long hair falling down one side of his chiseled chest, his features noble and strong.

The sight of him caught her breath, and she realized she'd been staring.

"Here," she said, thrusting the bundle of his clothes toward him.

He sauntered up to her, standing nude, only a foot between them. He made no attempt to take the items from her. She deliberately kept her gaze averted, her cheeks coloring with heat. She shoved them against his chest.

"Just take them, will you," she hissed.

He chuckled and finally relieved them from her grasp.

"We might as well rest up for a bit," he said, pulling the clothes on. "There's no point in us heading into the city before the others, just in case we get some unwanted attention."

She nodded. She guessed that made sense, though she was desperate to find out if Blake was safe.

The cool night air made her shiver.

"Come and sit with me," Chogan said, sitting down at the base of a large pine tree. The forest floor was covered in a soft bed of needles. "I'll keep you warm."

She didn't miss the cheeky smile on his face, but she couldn't say no. She'd freeze if she did.

She sat down beside him, and he slung his arm over her shoulder, like they were a couple of high school sweethearts. Deliberately, she kept her back angled toward him so as not to give him the wrong idea.

In an hour or so, they'd head to the outskirts of the city and grab a cab to take them to where she hoped Blake and the other shifters would be waiting.

THEY GOT THE driver to drop them off a couple of blocks from the meeting point. They walked the rest, side by side and in silence. Tension encompassed Autumn's entire soul, not just in anticipation of what might take place over the next few hours, but because she worried Blake wouldn't be waiting for her. Her heart thrummed, her breath shallow with nerves. She found herself clenching and unclenching her fists.

Please be there; please be there, she found herself chanting over in her head.

She glanced at Chogan and a slow smile spread over his lips. With a jolt, she remembered something Blake had told her about being able to send his wolf ahead of him to scout what lay further on. Had Chogan done that now? Had he already seen Blake waiting for them?

"Is he there?" she asked.

He only gave her a grin, which, with how Chogan worked, could have been either positive or negative.

"Tell me, damn it!"

He only smiled that knowing smile.

She gave a growl of frustration and broke into a sprint, rounding the corner where they were supposed to be waiting. Her heart dropped. No one was there. But then she caught movement from the alley right before the junction.

She almost burst into tears with relief. There was no possibility that the huge man standing, surrounded by a small group of people, was anyone else. His solid, indomitable form towered over the other men and women. Her heart beat hard, her mouth running dry. She wanted to run to him, but he'd told her he wasn't interested in her, that he couldn't think about her that way. Chogan lurked behind her, sandwiching her between the two cousins.

Blake must have caught sight of them in his peripheral vision. He turned his head toward them and a smile broke out on his face. Immediately, he left the people he was with, striding toward her. She held her ground, but he reached her and scooped her up, crushing her to him.

"Autumn! Thank God, you're safe."

Her arms found their own way around his neck, pressing her face into the strong curve of his throat, feeling his heat, drinking in the musky scent of him. His fingers laced in her hair and he pulled back her head, exposing her face to him, and kissed her, deep and sweet.

Whatever he'd said before, his actions now spoke differently.

She broke away from his embrace, her fingers automatically touching his cheek, his jaw, tracing down across his chest, back over his shoulders. "Are you all right?" she asked, part of her still feeling frantic. "Did they hurt you?"

"No, Autumn. I'm fine, honest."

"What happened back there? I heard gunshots. I was so scared."

He nodded grimly, his dark eyes locked on hers. "Yeah, I heard them too. I was worried you might have been shot, but once I'd managed to lose them, I doubled back and checked the direction you'd headed. When I didn't find any sign of blood, I figured you'd made it away safely."

As if his words had reminded him of the reason for her safety, he turned to Chogan. "Thank you for taking care of her."

The corner of his lip quirked. "No problem."

"So what happened at the reservation?" she asked, wanting to fill in every detail of their time apart.

"I let them catch sight of me and led them in the opposite direction of the one you'd all headed in. I found a spot near the river which was hidden from the aerial view by some boulders and overhanging trees, and managed to shift. Once I'd done that, I knew I'd be able to lose them."

"What about your father?"

Blake chuckled. "As expected, Dumas' men came to the house, but he threatened to pull a political shit-storm down on their heads because they were on reservation land, and they went away with their tails between their legs."

Autumn smiled. "Good. That's good."

They both became conscious of the people standing around them.

"There are still a few reporters hanging around the entrance," he said.

"Don't worry," said Chogan. "I can take care of them. Enyeto and I will take things from there."

"Okay." Blake turned to her. "Autumn, are you sure you're up for this?"

She nodded. "I want this to be over. I want my life back, or as much of it I can still get, and I'll do whatever I need to make that happen."

His lips tweaked in a smile. "Okay, then. You'll come with me."

"Damn right I am."

She didn't plan on letting him out of her sight again. Not knowing what had happened to him back at the reservation had felt like someone had ripped her soul in two.

Blake addressed the rest of the group. "And everyone else knows what they need to be doing?"

Heads were nodded, nervous smiles exchanged.

"We need to go to the subway station three blocks from here. Everyone, give us time to get there and then swing into action. Let's get our people back and teach these sons of bitches what they're dealing with."

A chorus of 'good lucks' rang out.

Blake took Autumn's hand and together they left the relative safety of the alley, and ran down the street.

CHAPTER TWENTY-TWO

CHOGAN PLANNED ON keeping the reporters busy, giving the others time to shift and make it up to the roof. Then the next part of the job would be down to them. Enyeto hung back, lurking around the corner until the time came for them to make their move.

He approached a redhead he recognized from the local news. She was young and beautiful, clad head to toe in a cream-colored Armani suit. She lifted a manicured hand to her mouth to stifle a yawn. Perhaps she wasn't used to being up this early? There was a reason he wanted her to notice him, and it wasn't purely so the others could enter the facility uninterrupted. If this whole thing went to plan, he intended to make sure things changed around here, and he would need her to make that happen.

With his hands shoved in his jean pockets, he sauntered up to her. "You're up early. So what's the latest?"

She turned, a frown marring her features, but then she caught sight of him, her eyes traveling up his body to rest on his face, and a smile tugged at her perfectly made-up lips.

"The news never sleeps." Her eyes flicked over his body again. "I assume you're not another reporter?"

He circled her. "No, I'm not another reporter, though I think I could have something which would make an interesting story for you."

"And what would that be?"

"Something related to the kidnapping you're all here to get the dish on."

Instantly her stance changed, her back straightening, eyes narrowing in suspicion. "And what would you know about it?"

"A fair amount." He paused. "Blake Wolfcollar is my cousin."

"Is this some kind of play for money? 'Cause you're talking to the wrong person. My producer is right over there." She nodded toward one of the news vans, where a man in his forties smoked a cigarette and nursed a take-out coffee.

"I'm not after money. I only want people to know the truth."

She cocked one eyebrow. "And you think you have the truth?"

"Hell yeah. And after today, none of you will ever look at life the same way again."

Now her expression changed to one of skepticism. Already, he could tell she was wondering if he was some kind of nut. The next hour or so would put an end to that.

Huge shadows glanced off the ground and the woman frowned and looked up. Chogan followed suit, lifting his face to the sky, though he already knew what he would see.

Two birds, giant eagles, rode eddies high above their heads, their sheer size only becoming apparent the closer they got. Mutters of astonishment turned to disbelief as the birds landed on the edge of the roof of the building, seeming to peer down at the gathering crowd. Early morning commuters joined the team of reporters in sky-gazing and people began to point and exclaim out loud.

"Holy cow!"

"Have you seen the size of them?"

"What are eagles doing in the middle of the city?"

"They can't be real!"

The reporter Chogan had been speaking to seemed to have forgotten he was there. The guy she'd pointed out to be her producer yelled, "Annabel, get your sweet ass over here! We need this on camera!" She left Chogan's side at a run, toward another man with a huge video camera. A third man holding a boom microphone ran behind him.

One of the birds let out an earsplitting screech and left the rooftop, plummeting through the air as it dived for the gathering crowd, huge talons spread. Chogan knew there was no way she intended on hurting anyone, but she certainly caught their attention. People screamed and lifted their arms to shelter their heads and faces. The powerful wings created a wind as she flapped to slow her downward descent and rise back into the sky.

From a distance came the now familiar thrum of helicopter blades.

Is it the same one that chased us before? Chogan wondered.

The chopper came into view over the building. It tried to land, veering and circling in the sky as if in some kind of mating dance with the two birds. Each time it neared the rooftop, one of the birds screeched and dived at the machine. If there was a collision, the two shifters would be killed, without doubt, but they would take the helicopter down with them.

Noticing the commotion, the security guards for the building came out, joining the crowd forming on the street. They'd not bothered to shut the darkened glass doors behind them.

Now was their chance. Chogan glanced over to where Enyeto was waiting and discreetly lifted his chin, giving him the signal.

With everyone's attention focused on the sky, they slipped inside the building.

BLAKE AND AUTUMN ran down the steps into the subway.
Blake paused and then tugged on her hand, leading her away from the trickle of commuters. "Come on, this way."

They left the main passageway and headed into a service tunnel. A metal gate barred the way, a thick chain and padlock keeping people out. Blake took the chain and lock in each hand and gave a huge wrench, bending the metal, forcing the lock to pop. He glanced to either side, checking the coast was clear, and then unhooked the chain and opened the gate. He pressed Autumn forward through the gap, then turned and pulled the gate shut again, looping the chain back through. The result wasn't perfect, but hopefully no one would notice the broken chain.

Any light from the train tunnel vanished as they went deeper. Blake's eyesight was better than a normal human's and his wolf's was excellent in the dark—sending him images to allow him to find his way. But Autumn had normal eyesight, and within a minute of entering this new tunnel, she started to stumble. He knew she couldn't see anything, despite the fact she hadn't complained, just clutched tighter to his hand.

"It's okay," he reassured her. "We won't be in the dark too long. We'll reach the facility soon."

"And then the real danger starts," she said, her voice coming out of the darkness. "I know the dark won't hurt me."

"I won't let anything else hurt you either."

She paused and said, "I just realized I have no idea who these people are we're about to try to rescue. Other than there are three of them and they're shifters, like you."

Blake got the impression she was using their conversation to ward away the imaginings which so often lay in the dark.

"One is a woman from the reservation," he told her. "She's from a different town, so I don't know her personally. The second is a man, white, like you. He has a family who must be missing him—a wife and two kids." He took a breath, hating to have to describe the third captive, understanding how coldhearted it must make him appear, to have left a boy in such a horrific situation. Even so, he continued. "The third is a teenage boy called Toby. He can't be much more than fifteen."

The pressure on his hand changed as Autumn slowed. "A teenage boy? His surname isn't West, by any chance?"

Blake frowned in the dark. "Yes, that does ring a bell."

"Now I understand why Mia is so involved. Toby West was her latest case."

"Damn."

Autumn's roommate had certainly gotten herself involved with the wrong people.

The tunnel twisted and turned, several junctions giving him options, which he took with no hesitation. Eventually, he came to stop.

A solid steel door blocked their way. A small keypad, illuminated by a pale blue light behind the keys, offered them their first light for a while.

"We'd better hope this works."

He tried to ignore the nerves in his stomach as he keyed in the code. The door beeped, the blue light turning green, and the door clicked open.

"Thank God," breathed Autumn.

Blake swung open the big, heavy door.

Ahead lay another tunnel, square in shape and lined with what appeared to be aluminum. He took up Autumn's hand once again and they ran at a steady jog down the sheer metal box. Overhead, florescent lights flicked on with their movement, only to extinguish again as they passed.

He wasn't sure what they'd find when they reached containment level three—whether the shifters would be protected by men with guns or if they'd even be there at all. But he knew Dumas' level of cockiness was high enough to never allow him to think someone would take him on—especially not a solitary man and a young scientist. In fact, that was probably the last thing Dumas would think he'd do. He imagined the men after them would expect them to try to put as much distance as possible between them and the facility.

They reached another slab of steel with another keypad. He plugged in the code and again the door opened. He'd been right, assuming Dumas to be too arrogant to consider Blake a threat. Either that or, as Blake had suspected before, the codes had deliberately been left unchanged, anticipating their return. In Dumas' mind, Blake was just a regular man. He had no idea about the common link Blake shared with the other shifters. Blake wondered what connection the general had made between him and Autumn. What did Dumas think his reason was for taking Autumn away? Blake didn't know how much information Haverly had given up, but he doubted his friend would have betrayed them. The general probably thought Blake wanted Autumn's power for himself.

This door opened into the back of containment level three, where the shifters were being held. A corridor led down into the room where the guards would be.

Using the hand that wasn't locked around Autumn's fingers, he reached back and removed his gun from where he'd hidden it in the waistband of his jeans. Before reaching the city, he'd gone back to where he'd stashed his bag of supplies a couple of days earlier and rearmed himself.

He wasn't expecting to find the shifters alone, and he wasn't wrong.

Blake peered around the corner. Two bored-looking guards sat on watch. He recognized neither of them. Had Dumas replaced some of his team after he'd taken off with Autumn? Perhaps the General figured he didn't know who to trust anymore and got fresh blood in, not wanting to leave anyone in charge who might betray him.

One guard chewed gum and idly flicked through his phone. The other sat with his feet resting on the control panel, his head back, his hands folded over his portly stomach. If Dumas caught them like that, he'd fire them in an instant.

He put out a hand to motion to Autumn to keep still. Her blue eyes locked with his, serious and alert, but not frightened. This wasn't some silly little girl he had with him now. She was a woman who'd fought to the top of her career and who, before the last couple of days, had known her place in the world. Now, her whole life had been flipped upside down, but she was still holding it together. He admired her for that.

Each of the doors to the glass cells holding the shifters were locked from the outside. When they released the shifters, they'd be able to make a run for it, but he worried about them being shot on the way out.

He wondered how the others were doing. They could set these shifters free, but they still needed to find Autumn's roommate. He also wanted to find out what had happened to Haverly and take out Dumas. The man wouldn't let them rest if he was left alive.

The one guard was so engrossed in his phone he didn't even notice Blake coming. Blake pressed the muzzle of his gun against the head of the man who appeared to be taking a nap. At the cold of the barrel, the man's eyes shot open.

"Don't move a muscle," Blake warned.

The other guard dropped his phone and scrambled for his gun, but Blake clicked the barrel forward, the sound loud in the otherwise silent place. The man gave a whimper of fear. "That applies to both of you."

The two men froze and exchanged a glance.

"Put your hands up where I can see them," said Blake.

He couldn't let himself be distracted by the three people held captive. First, he needed to deal with these two and make sure they didn't call for help. If they were anywhere else in the building, he'd be worrying about security cameras picking up on him holding these men at gunpoint, but the only cameras down here led to Dumas' office. With the commotion the others were hopefully causing in other parts of the building, he doubted he'd find Dumas sitting at his desk.

He motioned with the gun. "Get up and come over here."

The men scrabbled to their feet.

"Slowly," he said. Stepping forward, he quickly pulled both men's weapons from their holsters. He tucked one into the waistband of his jeans and kept hold of the other one. He figured Autumn would appreciate the weapon.

With both men in front of him, he called out, "Autumn, the boy is in the room farthest from you. Go and unlock it for me."

He allowed his gaze to move briefly to scan the two-inch-thick glass separating the room from the cells. He knew the shifters wouldn't be able to see through the one-way glass—their side was mirrored—but it was possible the stronger of the shifters, perhaps the man or woman, would be able to use their guides to see what was happening on the other side.

He was right. Though the boy lay curled up on his side, either asleep or unconscious, the man and woman sat up, alert, staring toward their mirrored side of the glass. They knew something was going on, though there wouldn't be any way for them to know he was here for them. As far as they were concerned, he was one of the guys on the bad team, and he needed to be prepared for the possibility that they would treat him like such.

From where he watched, the door at the back of the boy's cell swung open. Toby lifted his head. To one side of his body was a tray with an empty bowl and a plastic cup. At least Dumas had been feeding them. A bucket in the corner had served as a bathroom. From the way Autumn ducked her head back, her hand raised to her mouth, he guessed it hadn't been cleared in a while.

Through the microphone on the control panel, he could hear Autumn speak, "Hey, Toby, isn't it?"

The boy came to, caught sight of Autumn, and quickly sat up, scrabbling to the back of the cell.

She put her hand out, as though to a nervous animal. "It's okay. My name is Autumn. I'm here to help you, to get you out of here."

Toby's eyes darted around the small room, as though expecting to see some answer to what was occurring or figure out if this was a trick or not. His eyes seemed too big in his head, cheeks hollowed, arms thin. Whatever they'd been feeding him over the last couple of weeks, it either hadn't been enough, or he hadn't been keeping it down. Blake figured if Dumas had continued with his experiment, the resulting weight loss had probably been a mixture of both.

"You want to get out of here, right?" Autumn continued, one hand still held out. She crouched to his level. "My friend, Mia, runs a charity to find missing people, and your mom and dad contacted her. We're here to take you home."

Blake hoped to God that what she was telling him would come to fruition.

The boy looked around again. Apparently deciding he had no other options, he reached out and took Autumn's hand. Gently, she led him from his place of captivity.

"What the hell are you doing?" the guard with the belly yelled. "These people are dangerous. Hell, they're not even people!"

Blake cracked him on the side of the head with the muzzle of his gun. "Shut it, you."

Toby cowered at the raised voices.

The man in the chamber beside him started to hammer on his door. "Hey! Don't forget me! Get me out of here."

"It's all right," Autumn called out. "We're coming. Hang in there."

"Move, you two," said Blake, motioning with the gun toward the cell the boy had just vacated. "Get in there."

The guard touched the now bloodied spot on his forehead, wincing in pain, as he staggered toward the empty cell. "Oh, man, you've got to be kidding me."

"Just be thankful I've not shot you already."

He pushed the door shut on the two men and drove the lock home. Then he handed Autumn the spare gun. "Here, I figured you might want this."

"I've never shot anyone before."

"There's always a first time for everything."

She gave him a grim smile.

Banging from within the other two holding cells drew their attention. The captives' voices came, faint, but filled with desperation.

"I'll get this one," said Autumn, stepping forward and drawing back the huge iron bar from the middle cell. The door swung open and the woman with long dark hair almost fell out.

"Oh, thank God," she cried, stumbling into Autumn's arms. Tears of relief flowed down her dirt-streaked face, leaving tracks in their wake. "I thought I'd never make it out of that room."

"We're not out yet," said Blake. He opened the other room and the man also staggered out, clearly weak from lack of food and everything else that had been done to them. Burn marks marred the skin on each of their arms, healing crusts on abrasions from the cuffs they'd been kept in upon their arrival.

Blake hustled them back the way they'd come to where the door separated them from the metal tunnel.

"You need to go that way. There's a door at the end. The code is one-four-eight-six-one-nine. Do you think you can remember that?"

"Aren't you coming with us?" the woman cried, clutching Toby's hand.

He shook his head. "I can't. Other people are being held here who I need to find. Autumn, you can go with them if you want."

"Yes, please come," the boy pleaded.

"I'm sorry. My friend is in here somewhere. I have to find her."

Blake pulled the other gun from his waistband and handed it to the woman. "You know how to use this?"

She nodded, her eyes wide. "Then take it. If anyone from the unit tries to stop you from leaving, shoot them."

"Okay, I will." Her voice came out weak from emotion. "And thank you."

"Thank us when we see you on the other side."

She nodded, and with the man leading the way, the boy between them, they took off down the tunnel. Blake pushed the door shut behind them and something beeped, indicating the door had locked back into position.

"You ready for this?" he asked Autumn.

"As I'll ever be."

Together, they headed to the elevator. They stepped inside and Blake hit the button. His fingers found hers, holding hands as they waited for the elevator to rise and take them to their fates.

WITH EVERYONE'S ATTENTION focused on the craziness happening above their heads, Chogan and Enyeto had managed to slip inside the building, unnoticed. They ran around the metal detector, Chogan knowing he'd set off the alarms with the weapon he carried. Enyeto had no such weapon, his own special talent hidden.

Ahead of them, one of the sets of doors of a bank of elevators slid open. Blake and Autumn stepped out.

"Chogan!" said Blake, as he stepped out of the car and into the lobby. Chogan noticed the weapon held loosely at his side. "Is everything going to plan?"

"Everyone is focused on the roof. They did a great job. Where are the captive shifters?"

"They're already out. I sent them back the way I came in."

Chogan nodded approvingly. "Good job."

"Now we need to find Dumas."

The early hour meant the majority of the building's workers hadn't yet come in, however this was a twenty-four hour business and the facility was never going to be deserted.

From the corridor to their right, a man in a suit approached. "Hey, can I help you guys?" He did a double take on both Autumn and Blake, and recognition spread across his features. "Wait. You're … "

He started to back off, walking backward.

"I don't think so," said Chogan, not planning on allowing this guy to go and raise the alarm. He turned to Blake. "Go, we've got this. Find your friend and kill that asshole."

Within seconds, Enyeto crouched, a growl tearing through his body. His body began to swell and grow, doubling, tripling, quadrupling in size. From the tips of his fingers sprouted curved claws, a thick black fur covering what were now dinner-plate sized paws.

The huge black bear stood on its hind legs and roared, fragments of now destroyed clothes falling from its body. Chogan caught Autumn staring in a mixture of horror and awe as Blake pulled her backward into the elevator—the same expression he'd seen on her face when she'd first watched Blake and himself shift.

"Go," he told them again. "Go."

The elevator doors slid shut, taking Blake and Autumn with it. The sound of feet came running down the corridor. More security headed toward them, guns drawn.

They must have been spotted on security cameras, Chogan realized.

The men slid to a halt, shocked into non-action at the sight of the massive black bear now standing on its hind legs in the foyer.

"What the fuck?" One of the men gasped.

A couple of shots exploded in the confines of the building. One hit Enyeto in the shoulder, blood spraying out onto the floor. The bear let out another roar and ran at a huge, lumbering lollop toward the group of workers. They screamed in terror, a strange sound coming from so many big, strong men's mouths. A different security guy got off another shot, but the bullet went wide, hitting the glass separating an office from the corridor. Glass imploded inward, the woman behind screaming in fright.

Enyeto barely fit through the corridor, his big, bustling back end filling the space. Chogan followed, walking backward with his gun out held, literally covering Enyeto's ass. With the sound of the gunshot and breaking glass, the couple of guards who had left their post to go outside now came running.

"Hey, you there! Halt or I'll shoot!"

Chogan didn't give them time to shoot, squeezing off a couple of shots himself. One guard jerked back as he was hit in the shoulder. The other had caught sight of the huge bear and started to step away, clearly making his exit.

He knew they couldn't take out a whole department of people, and he didn't intend to, but they needed to create enough confusion and chaos to allow Blake time to find the man he needed to, and, if he could, Autumn's roommate as well.

CHAPTER TWENTY-THREE

MIA PEERED AROUND the small room she'd been locked in—some kind of storage closet, she suspected. The only light came from the shaft filtering from beneath the door. In the beam, she could just make out the man she'd been imprisoned with. He appeared to be a few years older than her, perhaps in his early thirties. Around his temples, flecks of white in his dark hair caught the small amount of light. His features seemed to be strong, though she struggled to distinguish much more. A white coat donned his body, similar to one a doctor would wear, though it had half fallen from his shoulders when he was thrown in here a little over an hour ago. An identification card was pinned to the pocket. She strained against her bonds to lean forward, trying to read the name on the card by the light from under the door.

P...something... Paul? Peter? She thought the surname might be Harvey.

The man worried her. He'd not regained consciousness, and she struggled to hear him breathing.

She tugged at the cable ties securing her wrists to some metal pipes on the wall. The plastic cut into her skin, so every movement felt like someone slicing into her wrists with a couple of blades. Pain shot up her arms and made her groan against the cloth wrapped around her mouth. The gag had grazed the corners of her lips and her tongue felt fat, her mouth and throat painfully dry. Her arms had been pulled behind her body for hours now, her shoulders aching, the muscles threatening to cramp.

She couldn't even begin to guess how long she'd been here. Every so often, a man in military uniform came in to give her a drink of water and place a bucket beneath her to pee, an experience almost as degrading as the kidnapping itself. The first couple of times, her bladder had frozen, refusing to relieve itself, but after numerous hours had passed and she'd even managed to sleep some, she'd woken to an almost painful need. That time, when the man returned, she'd been able to go.

At least no one had tried to touch her yet. That was her worst fear after the man who'd come to her apartment, Calvin Thorne, brought her here—wherever *here* might be. A cloth bag had been placed over her head, and she'd been bundled into the back of a van. She'd tried to keep track of which way they were heading, but after a couple of turns, she lost her sense of direction.

She knew what was happening to her now had to do with the missing boy, Toby. That she'd had her funding cut right after accepting the case wasn't a coincidence. Plus, strange men didn't warn you off a regular teenage runaway. But what she didn't understand—and what she couldn't figure out, no matter how many ways she turned things over in her head—was Autumn's connection in all this. She felt as though she was trying to put together a puzzle with half of the pieces missing.

She hoped her friend was all right. The man she'd seen briefly on the news looked like the same one Autumn described a couple of nights ago over dinner. She'd seen how Autumn's eyes lit up when she'd spoken of him. Her roommate was normally a pretty good judge of character. Would she really have been interested in someone who was actually a kidnapper and involved with men like Calvin Thorne?

None of it made any sense.

Muffled pops came from outside the room, like a distant car backfiring or firecrackers, but she knew deep down those weren't the reasons behind the sounds. Screams and men yelling followed, the slap of footsteps running down the corridor outside. Shadows flicked past the bottom of the door.

Mia tried to yell against the gag, but only managed to issue a muffled groan. Straining against her bonds sent fresh pain spiking through her body and she moaned again, her body heaving in a sob.

Somewhere in the building, an alarm went off, an undulating rise and fall of a wail.

Something was happening, but what? Did it have to do with her—someone coming to help her perhaps? Or was that just wishful thinking? She wanted to give herself a little piece of hope, but, as she had no idea what these people wanted from her, she struggled to see who the hell would even know she was here.

From the other side of the room, the man with the salt and pepper hair gave a groan. Mia sagged in relief. *Oh, thank God, he's not dead.* For a while, she'd started to convince herself she was locked in this room with a corpse, the idea threatening to snatch the final threads of control she had over herself.

The man moaned again and began to move. He rolled to his side and curled up in the fetal position before getting to his knees. He stayed in that position, his head hanging down, and gave another groan which sounded strangely like a growl.

The hairs on the back of Mia's neck prickled. Something wasn't right. She didn't just hear a growl, did she? The man began to twist and writhe, his shoulders jerking back and forth.

Oh God, they've put me in here with a lunatic! That's why they hadn't bothered to tie him up. They figured he'd kill her and save them a job.

A horrific sound, like flesh tearing, and an awful cracking filled the small space. Mia whimpered against the gag and instinctively squeezed her eyes shut, wanting to put her hands over her ears. *What's going on?* She forced her eyes open, making herself assess the situation. Though her insides had turned to water and she wanted nothing more than to curl up into a ball and try to pretend she was somewhere else, she thought doing just that would probably get her killed.

Staring into the dim light, her brain struggled to comprehend what she was seeing. The man's shape seemed to be changing, the texture of his skin completely different from anything she'd seen on a man before. Then he lifted his head, and his face ... *Oh God ... his face!* It no longer looked human, the jaw longer, sharp canines protruding from beneath the lower lip. Her eyes strained so wide she thought they might pop from her head. Surely this wasn't happening? She must have passed out and was now having some kind of crazy dream. Yet, if that was true, why did her wrists still feel like someone was slicing into them with razors?

The man continued to change, growing larger. Something whipped out from behind him. *Surely not a tail?*

His clothes fell from his body in tattered shreds.

She froze with terror, her breath trapped in her lungs. Bright amber eyes, lined in black, stared at her through the gloom, regarding her with something greater than human intelligence.

Mia tried not to pass out in the presence of the largest mountain lion she'd ever seen.

The animal trotted over to her.

Oh God. Please don't eat me, please don't eat me. She whimpered against the gag and shuffled back as far as possible, her back meeting with the pipes. But the big cat didn't snarl at her. Instead, it nudged her with its head, pushing her out of the way.

Oh no, it's going for the blood, she thought. *It can smell the blood from my wrists.* She wanted to fight back, but with her hands bound, there was little she could do. Heck, even if her hands *weren't* tied, this creature could rip her apart in less than a minute.

But instead of taking a chunk out of her hand, the cat started to chew on the cable ties attaching her to the pipe. *This isn't happening!* Hot breath warmed her skin, whiskers tickling the sensitive inner-wrists, sharp teeth grazing. She tried not to hyperventilate, her breath escaping her body in tiny, frightened gasps, stifled against the gag.

The cable ties suddenly popped, freeing her arms. Without allowing herself time to think yet, she yanked the gag from her mouth. Finally able to move, she had to stop herself from groaning in pleasure while she rolled her stiff shoulders and released the kink her neck had been suffering with for goodness-knows-how-long. She was so relieved she almost forgot about the giant mountain lion now sitting beside her, a low purr grumbling in its chest.

Almost.

"Oh shit, you're actually real, aren't you?"

The purring intensified in volume. From outside the door, more shots were fired. The cat got to its feet and padded to the door. It nudged the solid wood with its head.

"Really?" she said, still struggling to believe she was actually talking to a mountain lion. In a storage cupboard. Where there had been a man only minutes before. "Are you sure you want to go out there? Oh crap, what the hell am I talking about?"

She got to her feet, a rash of pins and needles flooding up through her toes and calves. Flexing her feet and legs as she made her way over to the door, she reached out and tried the handle. It wiggled, but the door didn't budge. The cat took a few steps back, and then leapt forward, barreling its shoulder against the door. The door bowed with a crash. The animal repeated the motion, again and again, while Mia stood out of the way as best she could, her knuckles pressed against her mouth. The door cracked and eventually splintered open. The big cat lifted its paws and padded through the hole, then turned back to her as if to say, "You coming?"

Mia stepped over the remaining shards of wood, careful not to catch herself. She found herself in a glass corridor she didn't recognize. A quick glance to her left and right, and she saw two men running toward her. Did she cry for help, or were these men involved in her kidnapping?

But as one got closer, she recognized the build and blond hair, and knew that if he got any closer she'd see gold flecks in his eyes.

Calvin Thorne.

"Jesus!" The security guard running at Calvin's side reached to grab his gun, but the mountain lion leapt, a tightly coiled spring of muscle, knocking him to the floor. The man's head hit the ground with a sickening crack.

Calvin Thorne reached for his own weapon.

"Watch out!" Mia cried.

With a snarl, the animal spun around, the movement fast enough to blur its golden fur. A swipe of its huge paw across Calvin's face rendered him either unconscious or dead, Mia couldn't be sure. He fell to the ground, gun clattering from his fingertips. Down the side of his face, five bright red lines bloomed and glistened.

If the man wasn't dead, he'd have some pretty fearsome scars to show for it.

The beast turned its head toward Mia and regarded her with those magnificent amber eyes.

She took a shaky breath. "Okay, I'll stick with you, shall I?"

It slowly lowered its head and then lifted it back up again. If she hadn't have known better, she'd have thought the animal had nodded.

CHAPTER TWENTY-FOUR

THE ELEVATOR PINGED open. Autumn recognized the floor as being the same one she'd come up to the morning of her interview with General Maxim Dumas. She could hardly believe the event had taken place only a matter of days ago. Her whole life had literally flipped on its head since then.

She glanced up at the man standing beside her and her heart swelled with emotion. It had only been a few days, too, since she'd first been introduced to Blake, and yet now she felt as though her life was in his hands, and there was no other place she wanted it to be.

Please don't let him get hurt.

She wanted them all to make it out of this alive. She wanted to know what the future had in store for them; if Blake would go back to his life on the reservation, or if he'd stay in the city with her. Where she'd lived her life so far surrounding herself in work, she now envisaged a life outside of the laboratory.

But with what was taking place here today, surely an inquiry of some kind would need to happen? After all, their names and faces had been all over the news. How could they tell anyone the truth of what actually occurred here without coming across as lunatics? Plus, if they ended up with blood on their hands, they would probably need to forget a future and head straight to prison instead.

At a light-footed run, they headed down the corridor, toward the office. The chaos on the other floors meant this one was now deserted of people. A couple of other doors stood open where people must have rushed out at the commotion. At the end of the hallway, a floor-to-ceiling window looked out onto an impressive view across the Chicago skyline. Autumn couldn't be sure, but she thought she glimpsed the swoop of a giant bird's wing block the view of the skyscrapers for the briefest of moments before vanishing again.

Her gun was still clutched in one hand, her palm slick with sweat against the metal. Blake locked eyes with her and motioned with his weapon to tell her to stand on one side of Dumas' closed office door while he took up position on the other side. Beneath them, somewhere in the building, came the sounds of gunshots and people's screams.

Autumn found herself praying for Chogan's safety. Though she didn't feel the same way about him as she did Blake, she couldn't pretend she felt nothing. He was special and had gone out of his way to help her, to help them. She wanted them to all be safe together at the end of this.

Blake mouthed at her, *"One, two, three..."* He jumped in front of the door, drew back his leg, and kicked the door open.

They both raced in, guns pointed. But other than Dumas' gleaming mahogany desk and a couple of other items of furniture, the room was empty.

"Damn it, where the hell is he?" Blake swore.

From behind, an arm wrapped around Autumn's throat and choked off the sound of her shriek. A cool circle of metal pressed hard against the side of her head as someone held her at gunpoint. Her heart rate leapt, pounding in her ears as she struggled to catch a breath. Her own weapon fell from her fingers and clattered to the floor.

"Don't move," Dumas breathed against her ear.

He'd snuck in behind them!

Autumn realized their mistake. They should have checked the rest of the floor was clear first.

Blake spun around, gun pointed.

"I wouldn't do that if I were you," said Dumas. "One step forward... In fact, if you so much as breathe in the wrong direction, I'm going to blow her pretty little head off."

"You wouldn't dare," said Blake, his eyes burning with anger. "You need her too much."

"Do I? Do I really? 'Cause the way I see it, I could blow her to pieces and simply mop up her blood to use. I can employ enough scientists to recreate whatever is in her blood that made the human DNA change. Then I'll have no use for her whatsoever."

"You'll have no use for her if you're dead. I promise you, if you harm her, I will track you down and rip you apart, piece by piece."

Dumas laughed, but his grip tightened around Autumn's throat, the muzzle of the gun jammed painfully into her temple. "Those are big words for a big man, I'll give you that much. But honestly, what do you expect to happen right now? That you'll threaten me and I'll just let her go running back into your arms? And what is this all about anyway? Why the sudden protection? I thought you loved your country, Blake. I thought you wanted us to succeed at this. Think of all the men you've lost in battle over the years. Wouldn't it have been so much better if they could have seen the enemy coming or if they missed something and were injured, that their injuries healed within a matter of hours so they could go back to their positions? Surely that is better than soldiers coming home as injured, broken men suffering from PTSD and no good to anyone?"

"I do want that, but not the way you're trying to achieve it, Dumas. Those people aren't freaks. They don't deserve to be treated as such. What you've been doing to them—to a woman, to a boy, for God's sake—is barbaric."

"So this has nothing to do with catching yourself a bit of blonde ass? It wasn't that you were worried our little scientist here was going to end up in one of the holding cells beside these people you suddenly care so much about? And please don't make out like you're some kind of innocent. You've been in the field, you know about taking sides and doing whatever is necessary for your country. You betrayed yours the day you decided to take the wrong side instead of working for your own."

"Those people are still American citizens! They deserve our protection."

"They're not even people. They deserve nothing!"

Blake gritted his teeth and Autumn watched him trying to get a grip on himself. Was she imagining things, or did she just see a ring of gold light glow from edges of his otherwise dark pupils?

"I don't care about any of that anymore," Blake said. "Just let Autumn go."

"Sorry, Blake. I liked you once, but you've betrayed your country. Now drop your weapon and kick it over to me."

"Don't do it, Blake," she managed to croak.

"Slowly," Dumas warned.

She saw the hesitation on Blake's features, the way his eyes darted over Dumas and herself, trying to figure out if he'd be able to get a clean shot. But even though Dumas was a tall man, Autumn was also tall, offering him almost full body protection.

"Damn it." With his free hand held up in surrender, Blake bent and dropped the gun to the floor.

"Now kick the gun over here."

Blake raised his booted foot and kicked the weapon so it slid over to stop at Dumas' feet.

Autumn's eyes flicked to where she'd dropped her own gun, the one stolen from the security guards. Perhaps Dumas wouldn't notice.

But he was too smart for that. Yanking her down with him in a choke hold that felt like her esophagus would be bruised for weeks, he ducked down and grabbed both weapons, tucking them into the waistband of his suit.

Dumas backed out, taking Autumn with him. He dragged her down the corridor.

Autumn battered at his arms. "Let go of me, you son of a bitch," she said, her voice hoarse.

"Shut up. Not a word or I'll do exactly as I said and blow your head off."

A familiar sound reached her ears, a cracking, followed by a howl of pain.

"What the fuck was that?" Dumas slowed, his head darting one way and then the next, trying to figure out where the sound was coming from.

The mournful howl of a wolf echoed down the corridor.

Oh no, Blake, don't do it, she prayed.

"What the fuck?" Dumas' arm loosened from around Autumn's throat, and she took the opportunity to slip from his grasp, and grabbed for the gun.

She felt the blast of hot air scrape her cheek before she heard the shot. The bang left her ear ringing and she fell to the ground, certain she'd been badly wounded. Behind her, she heard the crack of glass as the bullet punctured the window at the end of the corridor.

She just had time to touch her hand to her cheek before Dumas grabbed her again, hauling her to her feet. Her fingers came away bloodied, but she was relieved to find the wound to only be a scratch.

"You stupid little bitch," he snarled. "Don't you ever…"

His words trailed off as his eyes locked on something, widening in fear. From around the corner of his office door, a huge silver wolf prowled, dwarfing the corridor.

"What the…?" He started to take uncertain steps backward. Finally, the penny dropped. "Blake?"

The wolf lowered to a crouch and at leapt at Dumas. Dumas turned the gun from Autumn and fired, one, two, three times. Blake's body jerked with every shot, but he kept coming, blood dripping on the floor, and landed on Dumas, his massive paws planting on the man's chest, knocking him backward. Dumas flew back and hit the already damaged window at the end of the corridor. The window exploded in a thousand splintered pieces and the general vanished through the gap.

Just short of the gaping hole, Blake dropped to the floor.

"Oh God, Blake!" Autumn ran to his side.

Unconscious, his wolf's body shifted back to human, leaving him lying on the floor, bleeding and naked. A puncture wound gaped in his shoulder, another in his stomach, and a third grazed his bicep. The sight of the wounds made Autumn want to weep. *I need to get help!*

Movement at the opposite end of the corridor drew her attention and she lifted her head, tears blurring her eyes. Unsure of what she was seeing for a moment, she swiped at the tears, clearing her vision. But the thing she saw standing in the hallway didn't change.

A massive mountain lion regarded her with solemn, golden eyes.

She gave a cry of shock, forgetting what they were for a moment. But then a young woman raced around the corner, coming to a sudden halt right behind the beast.

"Mia!"

Her friend didn't show any reaction at the mountain lion. Instead, she ran past it, toward where Autumn was still crouched on the floor beside a now human Blake.

"Autumn! Oh, thank God you're all right."

Mia dropped to her knees beside her and they fell into each other's arms, tears rolling down both of their faces.

"What the hell is going on here?" asked Mia, pulling away. "I can hardly believe this is real." She focused on the naked, bleeding man on the floor and lifted a hand to her mouth. "Did you shoot him?"

"No! Of course not." She realized Mia had made the assumption from what she must have seen on the news. "Blake is one of the good guys."

An iron tang filled her nostrils. The sticky pool of blood forming on the floor beneath his body scared her, his skin turning pale, his breath shallow. "We need help. Do you have your phone?"

Behind them, the mountain lion snarled, pawing at its face as if something was bothering it. Bones cracked and the creature began to shrink, its ears folding back into its head, tail curling back in on itself to vanish between its legs. The fur melted from its body and the amber eyes darkened to a green-gray.

The man straightened.

Peter Haverly!

He stood naked before her, his body more thickly muscled than she'd ever given him credit for beneath the suit and lab coat. But in her mind, he was still her superior and the sight brought heat to her cheeks. She glanced over at Mia to find her staring, her dark eyes wide.

"There are phones in the offices," he said, already striding toward one of the open doors. "I'll call an ambulance."

The distant alarms in the building were overtaken by the wail of police and ambulance sirens from outside. Of course, someone would have seen Dumas' plunge from the window.

"It's okay," she said. "I think they're already here."

CHAPTER TWENTY-FIVE

IN THE CHAOS, Chogan slipped out and merged with the increasingly growing crowd. He hunched his shoulders and ducked his neck, trying to make himself as inconspicuous as possible. Cops barged past, trying, ineffectively, to force people to stay back while they entered the building. From what he could hear, they weren't yet sure what was going on inside, only that there had been a "disturbance" and possible gunshots fired.

He'd already sent a human Enyeto to the subway station Blake had told the captive shifters to run to. The bear-shifter had been instructed to take the others to the nearest police station, briefing them on the way about what to say—that General Maxim Dumas was the one responsible for their incarceration and subsequent torture. Though Chogan's instinct was to get the other shifters away from here, he didn't want Blake to be held responsible. They needed the testimonials of the captive shifters to clear his cousin's name. Plus, they should be reunited with their families and might even need medical attention. Chogan could do neither of these things.

He lay low, waiting for the initial uproar to disperse. After ten minutes or so, a couple of paramedics carried Blake out on a stretcher, handcuffed to the metal handle of the equipment. The sight tore Chogan. He wanted to make sure his cousin was all right, but he still wanted to complete his task. Blake locked eyes on him in the crowd, but said nothing. Autumn was hauled out right after, no handcuffs this time, but still with a cop holding her hands behind her back while she struggled and yelled at them to let her go.

A dark-haired girl and a slightly older man followed after, also flanked by police. The girl, teary-eyed and pale, kept shooting glances at the man as if she thought he might vanish.

A middle-aged man in a dark suit climbed the steps to address the crowd. One of the reporters pushed forward, microphone held in hand. "Detective Phillips, what can you tell us about what happened here today?"

The man shook his head. "Not much yet, I'm afraid. We can confirm there has been one fatality. Though the cause of death is probably from falling several stories down to street level, we're as yet unsure of the circumstances leading up to it. Several people have also been found with gunshot wounds, but, as yet, there are no further deaths to report. We're hoping it will stay that way."

"What about the reports of wild animals being on the loose?" the reporter asked. "Can you confirm if they've all been captured and where they came from? Did a zoo forget to lock its gates?"

The crowd gave a nervous chuckle at the comment.

Detective Philips didn't seem to find anything funny. He frowned. "So far, there have been no signs of any wild animals, despite numerous reports. We're currently assuming that part of what happened here was simply a hoax."

A murmur rose around the crowd, one of disbelief this time. Many of them had seen the giant eagles for themselves.

"Detective?" another reporter called out, but the man shook his head.

"That's it for the moment, folks."

He walked down the steps, hands held up as if in defense, as people bombarded him with further questions. He got into the passenger side of an unmarked car and the car pulled away from the curb, following already departed colleagues down the street.

Chogan took a deep breath, steadying his nerves, and jogged up the few steps to the entrance of the building. It dawned on him that he not only stood in place of the detective, but was also in the same position the silver-haired man he now knew to be General Maxim Dumas had been only a couple of days earlier. Behind him, a strip of yellow police tape barred the doors of the government facility.

More reporters had gathered, some giving live feed to the news channels. He spotted the redhead he'd spoken to earlier and deliberately made eye contact with her.

"Do you want that exclusive now?" he yelled.

She frowned, but nudged her cameraman and nodded over to him.

Happy the film was rolling, Chogan raised his voice and called across the crowd.

"I know you're all wondering what happened here today. Strange stories of giant animals—eagles, wolves, and bears. It's time the truth came out." He locked his eyes on the camera, speaking to the people beyond. "Those of you who are my brothers and sisters, you might have already guessed part of what happened here today. No longer should we be forced to live in the shadows, to hide ourselves away as though we're freaks. What happened in the building behind me is nothing short of an atrocity—shifters were being tortured! We should be the ones at the top of the food chain, the ones ruling the rest of humanity. Don't be ashamed of what you are any longer. Stand up, speak out, show them what you really are …"

A mutter came from the crowd. "The guy is clearly a loon."

The producer spoke to the reporter. "This is a freaking waste of time."

But the redhead shook her head. "No, wait. Just see what he's going to say."

"You can't be serious, Annabel?"

Chogan continued, unfazed by the negative comments. Another thirty seconds and they'd all be eating their words.

"Fellow shifters, take this footage and spread it far and wide. Upload it to every website, send it viral. Let everyone know what we are is real."

With that, he called his wolf to him. Its force soared toward him through the atmosphere. He lowered his head as it hit, a smash of energy. As always, his wolf was eager to shift. Where other guides might have been cautious because of what Chogan was attempting to do, therefore holding themselves back from the change, all Chogan's wolf wanted was to exist for real.

His neck cracked, pain searing through his body. The surface of his skin burned as though a million bees were stinging him. He gritted his teeth, bearing the agony by internalizing it—as he did every time—but by now they were beginning to elongate, his nose protruding as a snout. Ears uncurled from the top of his head and instantly his hearing grew sharper. Every joint in his arms and legs snapped, wrenching into positions they had never meant to take. Skin splitting at the base of his spine signaled the growth and unfurling of his tail. His body yanked and jerked, forcing him onto all fours.

Distantly, he was aware of the cries of alarm, shock, disbelief, horror even, rising from the crowd.

His clothes fell, unrecognizable, from his body. The change was complete.

Chogan lifted his wolf's head and howled.

CHAPTER TWENTY-SIX

AUTUMN SAT AT Blake's hospital bedside, her fingers linked with his on top of the white starched sheet, her eyes trained on his face.

He'd recovered consciousness when the ambulance had arrived, but then sunk back again in the back of the vehicle. He'd not woken again since.

She stared at the backs of his eyelids, at the network of light blue capillaries shielding his eyes, and prayed they would open. The sheet barely covered his naked torso, though bandages wrapped around his abdominals, chest, and across one shoulder where he'd been shot. Circles of monitors to trace his heart rate had been attached to his chest, and IVs plugged the veins in his arms.

The sight of him looking so vulnerable filled her with dread. What if he didn't recover?

No. She kept reminding herself of one of the reasons Dumas had been so interested in shifters—their ability to heal quickly. Blake was strong. He would come back from this.

The doctors said it was normal for his body to shut down in order to recover from the gunshot wounds. Plus, he had lost a large quantity of blood and was running a temperature of one hundred and four degrees, something Autumn suspected was down to his shifter genetics rather than the infection the doctors were treating with a high dose of IV antibiotics.

At least the handcuffs attaching him to the bed had been removed. The police had taken Autumn's statement, explaining how Blake hadn't kidnapped her—she'd gone of her own free will—and that Dumas' death was down to self-defense. That, together with the back-up statements from Peter Haverly, Mia, and the three captive shifters, explaining how Dumas had been the one to do the kidnapping, had quickly cleared Blake's name.

She had done her best to try to explain things to a baffled Mia. Her friend was relieved to learn Toby West was safe, though much of the rest of the story left her with her mouth hanging open in disbelief. Autumn noticed her incredulity hadn't stopped her friend from allowing Peter Haverly to take her under his metaphorical—in his case—wing. Mia, though stunned, didn't seem to mind the obvious interest he was showing her.

Autumn glanced down to see Blake's eyelids flickering. His fingers tightened around hers.

"Blake?" Her heart hitched in hope.

His eyes opened fully and she found herself with a stupid grin plastered on her face, her eyes brimming with tears.

"Autumn … you're safe." His voice came out as a croak. "You're here."

She squeezed his hand, her voice choked with emotion. "Where else would I be?"

His eyes locked on hers. "What happened?" As he spoke, he seemed to grow stronger.

"You were shot. They brought you to hospital, remember?"

But he shook his head. "No, I mean what happened with Chogan? What did Chogan do?"

She didn't want to tell him, worried the news would set his healing back. Earlier, the small television mounted on the wall in the corner had been on, feeding the news report into the room. She'd switched the box off, unable to stand to watch any longer. Terrified about what it might mean.

She bit her lower lip, shaking her head.

His fingers squeezed hers, hard, almost on the verge of pain. "What did he do?" His voice was a growl.

She knew she had to tell him. "He's tried to expose you all. He shifted on camera, in front of a live news crew."

His eyes darkened and he pushed himself to sitting. "That goddamned idiot. I knew he'd try to pull something like this." Blake reached down and tugged the sensors off his naked chest, sending the monitors into a beeping frenzy.

"What are you doing?" she asked in alarm.

"Damage limitation." He yanked the drips from his arms, bright red blood welling in the holes that had previously been plugged, trickling down his wrist.

"Blake, you've been shot. Stop that! You need to rest."

He swung his legs off the side of the bed, and despite the circumstances, she couldn't help but admire the powerful, thick thighs on display. "I can't. God knows what sort of shit storm Chogan has stirred up."

She shook her head, frantic. "It's okay. People don't believe the footage is real. They're saying it's a hoax and the news crew and other eye witnesses were paid off."

So far, the human nature of trying to rationalize anything not understood had kicked in, and rather than thinking what had happened was real, theories of magic tricks and video doctoring were being batted around.

"It doesn't matter. There will be other shifters who he's reached out to who will see the footage and agree with him."

Called by the monitor alarm, a couple of nurses, followed by a doctor in a white coat, came rushing into the room.

"Where are my clothes?" Blake demanded.

The doctor frowned. "Mr. Wolfcollar, what do you think you're doing?"

"Getting out of here, that's what. Now get me my clothes!"

Autumn had gathered the clothes he'd been wearing before he'd shifted from Dumas' office, knowing he'd need something to wear when he got out. It appeared as though he'd managed to kick off his boots and get his jeans half-off before he'd shifted, but his white t-shirt was basically in tatters. At least he hadn't been wearing clothes when he'd been shot, so eliminating gun holes and blood from them.

However, the reason for his nudity had been difficult to explain to the paramedics. Now, what remained of the jeans, t-shirt, and boots were folded in the small closet in the corner of the room.

Autumn grabbed the items and handed them to him with an almost apologetic smile, though she had no idea what she was supposed to be sorry for.

Blake pulled on the tattered garments, the muscles of his thighs glimpsed between the tears in his jeans, the shredded t-shirt exposing his thickly muscled chest and biceps. The bandages he wore offered more covering.

The result was almost erotic and Autumn swallowed hard.

Blake glanced down at himself as if wondering if he could get away with the attire, and then gave his head a brief, dismissive shake. Clearly, he figured he had more important things to worry about.

"Mr. Wolfcollar," the doctor said, in an authoritative voice, trying to stay calm though two high spots of color bloomed in his cheeks. Blake towered over him by at least a foot. He wouldn't be able to physically force him to stay. "If you discharge yourself from this hospital, I want you to know that you are doing so against medical advice. Should something go wrong, we won't be held responsible."

Blake glanced at the man as if only just realizing he was there. "Don't worry, Doctor. I won't sue, if that's what you're worried about."

He grabbed Autumn's hand, and together they left the room and hurried down the halls of the hospital.

"Where are we going?" she asked, glancing worriedly at the spots of blood which had appeared on the bandages and against the white of the remains of his t-shirt.

"To find Chogan."

"I thought this whole thing was done with now. Now that Dumas is dead and the others are free." After everything they'd been through, surely now they'd be able to have some peace, to try to get their lives back to some kind of normality, whatever that might be.

But Blake shook his head and turned to look at her, drowning her in those deep, dark eyes she'd grown to love.

"No, Autumn. This is only the start."

Like what you've read?

Make sure you sign up to Marissa Farrar's new release list to stay updated about new releases, exclusives, and special offers!

NOTE FROM THE AUTHOR

This book is a work of fiction, and as such I have taken liberty in some of the names used for my Native American characters in order to fit their guides. Big Lake Reservation is a fictional reservation, but in the area in which the reservation is set there is a real reservation named Red Lake Reservation. This reservation is Sioux, and while I have not specified what type of tribe my own Native American characters have come from, I'm aware that I have used different meanings from different languages from different tribes over the course of the book.

I hope you will forgive me.

Marissa.

ACKNOWLEDGEMENTS

As much as writing a book can be a solitary process, the publishing of a book is anything but. As always, I would like to thank the little team of people behind me who help turn my manuscript into a novel to be proud of. Huge thanks to my editor, Shontrell Wade, for always managing to stick to my sometimes tight publishing schedule. On this occasion, we had the birth of a baby to try to beat! Thanks to my proofreader, Lori Whitwam, for your sharp eye and kind words. And thanks, as always to my mum, Glynis Elliott, for being a stickler for grammar and my first reader.

I also need to thank my family for putting up with me getting crazy during the editing process, and for putting up with a messy house and frozen dinners during the writing process. Thanks to my husband, Rick, for whisking the kids away when I need just a few hours peace to get things done. This writing adventure would mean nothing without you guys.

And finally, thanks to you, my readers, for all your words of encouragement and constant support. You've all helped make my dream of being a full time writer a reality.

If you want to stay updated about my new releases, please sign up to my new release list on my blog. You will receive notification of when a new book comes out, together with exclusive previews and sales!

www.marissa-farrar.blogspot.com
Thank you once again.

Marissa.

ABOUT THE AUTHOR

Marissa Farrar is a multi-published fantasy and horror author. She was born in Devon, England, has travelled all over the world, and has lived in both Australia and Spain. She now resides in the countryside with her husband, soon-to-be three children, a crazy Spanish dog, two rescue cats, and six hens. Despite returning to England, she daydreams of one day being able to split her time between her home country and the balmy, white sandy beaches of Spain.

Even though she's been writing stories since she was small and held dreams of being a writer, her initial life plan went a different way.

In her youth, inspired by James Herriot, she decided to become a vet, and would regularly bring home new pets to her weary parents. Upon discovering her exams were never going to get her into a veterinary degree, she ended up studying Zoology. Once she completed her degree and realised she'd spent the majority trying to find time to write, she decided to follow her dream of being an author. Seven years later, she was published and two years after that she was able to say goodbye to the day job.

However, she's continued to collect animals!

Marissa is the author of four novels, including the dark vampire 'Serenity' series. Her fifth novel, *Underlife*, a dark fantasy set beneath the streets of London, will be published September 2012.

Her short stories have been accepted for a number of anthologies including, *Their Dark Masters,* Red Skies Press, *Masters of Horror: Damned If You Don't,* Triskaideka Books; and *2013: The Aftermath,* Pill Hill Press.

If you want to know more about Marissa, then please visit her website at:
www.marissa-farrar.blogspot.com.

You can also find her at her facebook page,
www.facebook.com/marissa.farrar.author

or follow her on twitter @marissafarrar.

She loves to hear from readers and can be emailed at
marissafarrar@hotmail.co.uk.

www.ingramcontent.com/pod-product-compliance
Lightning Source LLC
Chambersburg PA
CBHW051502170626
46811CB00002B/608